AF415115

Obsidian

Rigby Brothers

S L Davies

Published by S L Davies, 2022.

This is a work of fiction. Similarities to real people, places, or events are entirely coincidental.

OBSIDIAN

First edition. September 14, 2022.

Copyright © 2022 S L Davies.

ISBN: 979-8201045678

Written by S L Davies.

O bsidian

I sighed as I watched over my nephews and nieces as they played. They ran about the backyard at my parents' house laughing and chasing one another. Iver had organized a game of tag and was teaching Drake and Arsen's daughter, Whisper, to pursue after Bear, who was currently shifted, and let the others chase him. Whisper had just started to walk and watching Iver and how gentle he was with her was so cute.

All of my brothers other than Jericho now had mates and children. Jericho said he didn't care if he never found someone. But I didn't feel the same. I'd always wanted a mate. I remembered when Bacchus saw Anghus and how they almost broke apart because they were two alphas. Then when they found Joachim, it seemed to complete them. Apart from the slight hiccup with a thought that Joachim and Anghus could have been related. But once that was found to not be true, they were inseparable.

I remember speaking to Bacchus and being horrified that Anghus would consider walking away from his mate. I could never have done it. I've wanted a mate for as long as I've known what they were. We had grown up in a fantastic house. Mama and Papa never hid their love. I wasn't naïve enough to think it was all sunshine and lollipops. I was sure there were times that they had trouble or disagreements. But for the most part, they were happy. Their love was evident.

I desperately wanted it. But I felt like I was never going to get it. Even Macklin, the grumpiest of us all, had found a mate and was in love. I was never hard up for sex, which came easy. But it wasn't sex that I wanted. I wanted someone that I could call my own. I wanted my mate. I'd asked the creator so often to send me a mate. But still, I didn't have one.

"What's crawled up your ass?" Jericho asked as he sat down beside me and bumped my shoulder.

I thought I'd been hiding my grumpiness, but obviously not well enough. But then again, Jericho had always been the most observant of my brothers.

I sighed. "I want that," I said, nodding my head to the backyard, where my brother Asher shifted into his bear form and allowed the kids to climb over him. Whisper threw her head back and giggled as Iver lifted her onto Asher's back and held her so that Asher could take her for a ride.

"Why?" Jericho asked.

"Don't you get lonely, man? I mean, I can't help but think how much happier they all are with someone they get to come home to. Their kids seem to make them smile a lot more."

"Yeah, but then they don't get to go out whenever they want. They have to be responsible and grow up."

I shrugged my shoulders. "I don't see the bad side to that."

"Really? You want to give up all your midnight booty calls to settle with one?"

I sighed and nodded my head. "Yeah, man, I do. Don't you get tired and sick of chasing tail all the time? Wouldn't you rather settle down, knowing that the one you love is there for you?"

Jericho shrugged. "Na. Not really. I mean, sometimes I think about it. Especially when I'm by myself at home. But I don't know. I'm not sure my life is meant for someone to be in."

"Why?"

Jericho shrugged again. "Dunno. I mean, it's not like I'm home all that often. I work weird hours. My job isn't really made for a successful relationship. Lots of the guys have had relationships, and they never end up working because of our hours."

I nodded. "Yeah, I suppose."

"Don't worry so much. You will find someone. I know you will. Have you tried asking Iver?"

I shook my head and chuckled. "Na. I don't want to use the kid as a party trick for my own use."

"You know he doesn't mind."

"I know. Maybe I don't want to know if the answer is that I'm never meant to have someone."

"I don't believe that. I think there is someone out there for you. They will come when you least expect it."

I smiled over at Jericho. "You trying to take on Iver's role?"

Jericho grinned and stretched in his seat. "Someone has to pull you out of this dark cloud you've been lingering in."

"Have I been that bad?" I asked with a wince.

Jericho smiled and shook his head. "Na. Not really. I don't think the others have really noticed, but I had. You haven't been as smiley and playful lately. Mama had noticed too."

I nodded my head. If Mama noticed, that meant she had sent Jericho to give me a slap under the ear and tell me to buck up.

"I'll give Mama a big bear hug and a kiss and apologize."

Jericho chuckled. "See to it that you do," he replied with a wink before climbing off the back deck. He aimed up Anghus and leaped into the air, tackling the gargoyle to the ground. Anghus grunted and caught Jericho as they began to wrestle.

"Go, Dad," Iver yelled. "Don't let him take you."

I chuckled as I watched their shenanigans. I was fortunate to have the family I had. I shook my head. Enough moping. I stripped out of my clothes and called my panther forward. Crouching low, I stalked down the back stairs and moved slowly towards where Jericho and Anghus were still wrestling.

"Go get 'em, bro," I heard Asher chuckle through the link. I crept closer, timing my leap.

I got within inches of my brother just as he turned and spotted me. His eyes widened, but they danced with humor as he screeched and jumped off Anghus before landing heavily on my back and clinging to me as I rolled to my side with a grunt. I chuckled and lay in the sun as the kids piled on me.

Chapter One

P^{itt}

"Are you sure you have everything?" Papa asked as he looked me over. My car was packed, and I was about to head off. I was nervous but needed this. It was time to grow up and move out on my own.

"I'm sure I have," I said as I glanced over at my car while biting my bottom lip. I didn't know where I was going. I didn't have a plan, which was probably the most stupid thing I'd ever done. But I needed this. I needed to heal. After losing yet another job because of my anxiety, I needed to get away.

"And you got your car looked at?" Dad asked as he stood beside Papa.

I nodded my head. It was a lie. I hadn't. I didn't have the money to get my car serviced. It was either paying for fuel to make this insane trip or getting my car looked at. I'd chosen instead to ignore the rattle that my vehicle had going on and go on this trip.

"I'm worried about you," Papa said. "Are you sure you are going to be alright?"

I nodded my head. I wanted to burst into tears and say no. I wanted to hide and not come out. But that had never done me well. Hell, I couldn't even keep a job because of my fears. Irrational fears at that.

"I will be alright. I'll ring you every day," I promised, putting on a brave face.

"No matter the time or where you are, if you need us, ring. We will come and get you or find a way for you to come home," Dad promised.

I blinked back the tears that were forming and nodded. "Thank you," I croaked.

"Oh baby," Papa said as he pulled me into his arms. "I'm so damned proud of you."

That was all it took. The tears I'd been bravely pushing to the side started to fall, and I hiccupped a sob as I questioned again whether I was doing the right thing. I'd always been a nervous kid; even when I was little, I struggled with separation anxiety from my family. I often stuttered when I talked, could barely speak to strangers, and hated being the center of attention. As I grew, my nervousness became full-blown anxiety to the point that I could no longer attend school.

I'd had so many jobs to break free of the anxiety. I'd see therapists and take all the medication. But it didn't seem to make a difference. It wasn't until my therapist, Naomi, suggested I go for a holiday somewhere. I think she meant just a few days in a hotel somewhere. However, my brain didn't work like that. I'd got it in my head that I would travel around Australia. Sleep in my car and do odd jobs for money.

I'd planned out my budget, but not the actual trip, I'd decided that it would be more fun to be spontaneous. Then I lost my job at a restaurant when I screamed as a man touched me. I didn't mean to; I just hadn't realized he was behind me. However, it had a knock-on effect. I screamed, he shouted and jumped, stumbling into Mark, the waiter carrying a glass of wine, spilling on another customer, who got angry and yelled at Mark.

My boss, Dorothy, ultimately told me I could no longer work there. I understood it as much as it was a blow to my confidence. But I didn't blame her. There was no way that I could continue working in a place where I became a danger to customers.

"I'll be alright," I said again to reassure myself as well as Papa who looked like he was on the verge of putting his foot down and demanding I stay home.

"Remember what we said, you ring at any time, and we will be there to help you," Dad said as he pulled me into his arms and kissed the top of my head.

Some may say I was spoiled as the youngest of the Stein children, but the truth was that Dad and Papa had loved all of their children equally. My eldest brother Nathan was already mated to a wonderful man named Christopher. Nathan had gone on to become a surgeon while Christopher was a nurse. Together they had six children. Each of the kids was just as spoiled as we had been. Then my older sister Talia and brother Carson lived in Melbourne. Talia was a graphic designer, while Carson was a real estate agent. They were yet to be mated, but I don't think they were in any hurry. And then there was me. The fuck up. Well, no, I couldn't really say that. It wasn't exactly my fault my brain didn't work like other people.

I pulled away from Dad and opened the car door with a creak. "I love you both," I said with a smile as I brought the engine to life with a rattle. Dad winced, and I could tell he wasn't convinced my car would make it.

Dad and Papa had offered to buy me a new car. All of my siblings had new cars bought for them on their eighteenth birthdays. But I hadn't wanted a new car. I liked the old Valiant that I saw. It had been owned by one man since brand new. In my eyes, she was beautiful. While others looked and saw a broken old car, I saw beauty. She reminded me of me. But her engine was old and tired, and I wasn't sure she would last all that long. I just hoped she would last long enough to get me somewhere I could work for a bit and earn enough money to get her fixed up.

With a final wave, I pulled out of the driveway of my childhood home in Croydon in Melbourne and took off for destinations unknown. I breathed in deeply as I pointed Valerie, my car's name, towards the Western Freeway and started my journey.

Chapter Two

O bsidian

"Uncle Sid, where are you?" Iver yelled from the shop office. I rolled out from beneath the car I was currently working on and grinned up at my nephew staring down at me.

"Iver boy, is it already two?" I asked. I sat up, pulled the rag from my back pocket, and wiped it over my face.

Iver nodded his head before he giggled. "You just made it worse, Sid," he said before taking the rag from me and wiping my brow where I had a smear of grease.

"Thanks, kid. Papa in the office, is he?" I asked.

"Yep. McKenna didn't come; she wanted to stay with Daffodil and Royal."

I placed my hand to my chest and gasped in pretend hurt. "I'm wounded. My niece would rather spend time with her cousins than her favorite uncle."

Iver giggled and reached out a hand to help me stand from the trolley I was sitting on. "So what tatt are we getting today?" he asked.

I'd promised Iver that I would take him to Shifter Ink when I got my next lot of art from Burgess. Iver was going to get a tattoo also. A fake one, but until his Papa finally convinced him to wash it off his back, Iver had a tattoo.

"Well, I'm getting more work down on my back. What have you got planned?" I asked.

"I'm going to get a kraken on my back."

"Nice. Your Dad will love that," I said. My brother Bacchus was a kraken shifter. Iver grinned and nodded his head. "Who have you convinced to do your work for you?"

"Sloane," he answered. "She's the best at doing old school."

I chuckled. All my nephews and nieces loved going into Shifter Ink to get their tattoos drawn on with sharpies. Burgess adored all of them, as did the other tattoo artists.

"Well, then let's get going," I said as I walked over to the sink and looked in the mirror to ensure I'd got all the grease off my face. I quickly scrubbed my hands. Not that it was getting rid of all the motor oil that stained my fingers and fingernails. That would take months of manicures to fix that mess. It was part of being a mechanic. I remembered that about Papa growing up; he always had grease-stained fingers. Unlike Asher, whose fingers always looked manicured and soft.

I walked with Iver into the office where Anghus was sitting with Alena and Donte, one of my mechanics and a member of the Devil's Advocates. He was also Asher's brother-in-law. I swear that the way my family interweaved with everyone in town was getting more complicated.

"Tattoo time?" Donte asked.

I grinned and nodded my head. I had a regular appointment with Iver every fortnight. We all took turns in having the kids with us during the weeks. It was our way of giving our brothers and their mates a break but also a chance for us to spend time with our nephews and nieces. I loved it. Even though I was an alpha, and the stereotype was that alphas weren't paternal, that was different for me. I would give anything to have kids of my own. One day. Hopefully.

"Be good for Sid," Anghus said, pointing at Iver, who grinned at his father. The kid looked just like my brother Bacchus. His eyes sparked the same with mischief. But he was so much like Anghus in his personality. Iver could be so serious that sometimes it was easy to forget that he was still just a little boy.

"Iver's always good. What are you talking about? He isn't like you, Anghus; he is good," I said.

Iver threw his head back and barked out a laugh. Anghus smirked and held his hand out to shake mine.

"Don't teach him anymore swear words," Anghus warned, causing me to chuckle.

So, I may have a bad habit of swearing when things went wrong in the shop, and I may or may not have inadvertently taught my nephews and nieces some bad words that they went on to use in front of their parents. Thankfully my brothers loved me and hadn't killed me yet.

"Can't make any promises," I said with a laugh as I led Iver out of the office and towards my car. "Let's get us some tatts, and then I reckon we deserve a burger."

"Yes," Iver said with a cheer as he climbed into the passenger side of my car and buckled his seat belt.

I chuckled and brought the car to life with a roar. My Mustang was my baby. I'd got her from an old guy that had left her in his shed for years. After replacing the engine and the interior, I was in love. She was my pride and joy; I'd be lost without her.

Chapter Three

P^itt

I was singing, well, I guess some may call it howling, as I sped along the freeway to destinations unknown. ACDC played loudly. The window was down, whipping the breeze through my long hair. I felt a sense of freedom. It had taken me a couple of hours before I finally started to ease into what I was planning on doing. I'd turned off the Western Freeway and decided to head towards the coast and follow it. My stomach started to growl, and when I glanced at the time, I realized that it was after lunch, and I hadn't eaten anything since leaving early that morning.

Glancing up, I noticed an offramp and a sign to a town called Lalbert. I slowed for the exit and pulled off, following the signs to Lalbert. I had never been really outside of Melbourne. Dad and Papa used to take us down to Port Phillip Bay in the summer to swim in the ocean occasionally. Still, we swam in the Yarra River most of the time and didn't travel. We didn't need to. We had everything we needed at home.

The open plains of farms changed to the forest until I was driving along tree-covered roads, with woods on either side of me. The scenery changed the more I went towards where the signs for Lalbert sent me. The sign told me I had about five kilometers before I got to Lalbert. There was a little knife and fork picture on the town sign, so I knew I could expect to find something to eat there.

Suddenly Valerie started to sputter. I looked down at the fuel gauge, but it was still reading that I had plenty of fuel. A loud bang sounded, and steam started pouring out of the bonnet. I edged Valerie to the side of the road and popped the hood.

"Shit," I groaned. I had hoped we would make it a lot further into the journey before I had to ring Dad. Sighing, I climbed out of the car. Steam spluttered, and I sighed again. It wouldn't matter how long I stood there looking at it; I wasn't going to know what was wrong with it.

I plucked my phone out of my pocket; maybe if I could find a mechanic in the area, I might be able to get it fixed. I winced as I thought about how much it would cost me. Maybe I could work off the cost. I chewed on my bottom lip as I looked down at my phone and realized I didn't have phone coverage.

"Shit," I swore again. How fucking typical of my life. I glanced up the road; the sign had said five kilometers, which had to be about a kilometer ago. I could walk and hope that I found someone. But then, my luck, it would be a one-horse town, and the only thing in the whole place would be a pub or a general store.

I bit further into my lip, scraping at the skin anxiously. My heart started to pound in my chest and sweat began to bead along my brow. I knew my anxiety would kick off if I didn't find a solution soon. I couldn't even ring Dad. Not without phone coverage. I walked back to the car's driver's seat and popped open the glove box. I pulled my bottle of pills out and popped one out before swallowing it down. That would hopefully take the edge off my panic attack before it became uncontrollable.

Suddenly I heard the roar of an engine, and when I looked up the road, I noticed a motorbike heading towards me. I didn't know what to do. *Should I flag them down?* Maybe they could give me a lift into the nearest town. They were heading towards Lalbert; perhaps they would know I could get help somewhere. The closer the motorbike got to me, the more I panicked. I hadn't decided if I should flag them down or not. However, the decision was quickly taken out of my hands as the motorbike pulled up behind my car.

A tall guy with dark hair and an MC cut climbed from the bike. My whole body was trembling with fear as thoughts of what might happen to me went through my head. *What if he wasn't there to help? What if he wanted to kill me?* He was part of an MC, which could mean I was in danger.

My vision started to blur, and panic began to take over. Tears started filling my eyes, and my breath became choppy. I knew that if I didn't calm down, I would faint, which would be bad; it would mean that I would become utterly vulnerable to the stranger.

"Hey, it's alright; I'm not here to hurt you," the man said quietly. He didn't come close to me but stood at my car's boot.

"I... I... I. bbbbroke down," I stuttered.

"Okay, I'm a mechanic. But I can see you are struggling with panic right now," he said. I nodded my head as tears trekked down my cheeks. What a way to meet a local. "I'm going to come and look at the engine; I'll go around the other side of the car, okay?"

I nodded my head again as I tried to slow my breathing down and allow the valium I'd just taken to start to work. Slowly I blew out a breath and began tapping on my leg as I tried to work through the relaxation techniques Naomi had shown me.

My heart rate started to decrease, and I could get a hold of the tears and calm them down. I breathed in and out, concentrating on each breath. Finally, once the anxiety eased, I could turn and face the man looking under my bonnet.

"Thank you," I said quietly.

The man looked up at me and smiled. "Not a problem. I think you have done a head gasket and a water valve. I work in Lalbert at a mechanic called Obsidian Mechanics; I can organize a tow truck. I can't ring from here though cause I've not got coverage, but about five hundred meters up the road, I get coverage back."

I nodded my head. "That would be good. How much will it cost?" I asked quietly.

The man shook his head. "Don't worry about that now. We can do payment plans and stuff, so you will be alright. Do you want to ride with me or wait for me to return? I'll go up there and call Obsidian and then come back."

"I... I... I'll wait here," I stuttered, still feeling the residual of my anxiety.

"No worries. I will be right back," the man said.

"Wait. What is your name?" I asked.

The man grinned. "Donte. How about you?"

"Pitt," I replied.

"It's great to meet you, Pitt. Sit down and relax; I won't be a minute."

Chapter Four

Obsidian

"Ouch, fuck ya," I grunted as Burgess hit a sensitive area near my spine.

"Sit still and stop being a pussy," Burgess spat back. I loved my brother's tattoos, but I swear he kept his roughest style for when I came in.

Iver was currently laying on Sloane's table with his eyes closed and a serene smile on his face as she drew over his back with sharpies. At least he wasn't getting his brother to stick him with needles in the spine.

"Fuck, man, I'm sure you've done that part already," I groused.

Burgess laughed and lifted his hand. "I don't know why you bother getting tattoos; you complain every time. If you can't take the pain, don't get them."

"Or get them somewhere really fatty," Sloane said.

"He doesn't want tattoos on his head," Iver mumbled.

I stared at my nephew with wide eyes as Burgess and Sloane erupted into seizures of giggles.

"What the fuck, man? You're meant to be on my side," I grumbled.

Iver opened his eyes, and his grin matched the cheeky look. "What was it Dad said about swearing?"

I rolled my eyes and huffed. "Geez, when did you turn on me?"

Iver snorted. "I still love you, Uncle Sid; I'm just playing."

I winked and grinned. "Just as well, or I'd have to eat burgers all by myself."

Iver's eyes widened, and he gasped. "You would do that to me? Your favorite nephew?"

"I dunno; I think Thatcher is looking a lot more loveable," I said with a laugh.

"Oh no, you don't. You will not bring my son into this; he has already learned enough swear words from you," Burgess said as he pushed me back onto the table and started tattooing again.

"He never used it outside the house," I complained.

"No, he just called his sister a cunt," Burgess muttered, causing me to laugh.

"I've already apologized for that."

"And I'm yet to forgive you."

I not only went home with fantastic artwork on my skin but always came away with a smile and aching jaw from laughter. This was what I loved about coming into Shifter Ink and getting tattoos from my brother. It was an excellent chance for us to catch up where he wasn't having to think about being a Papa. Instead, he could just relax and be himself.

My phone started to buzz in my pocket. "Want me to stop so you can get that?" Burgess asked.

"Yeah, it might be work," I said as I wrestled my phone from my pocket and looked at the screen to see that it was Donte calling. He'd left the shop after I did so that he could pick up a few parts for me.

"Donte, did you get the parts?" I asked.

"Yeah, I did. Listen, I've got a guy on the side of the road, broken down in an old but beautiful Valiant. Looks like he's blown a water valve and a head gasket. I was hoping you were done and could bring out the tow truck," Donte said.

"Na, I'm still at Shifter Ink. But I'll give Dakota a call; he will be able to bring it out and hook it up. Where are you?"

"On Lalbert road, about four k out."

"Alright, I'll ring you back in a sec," I said before ending the call and finding Dakota's number. He was one of my other mechanics; if I wasn't around, he usually drove the tow truck if needed.

"Hey, Sid," Dakota answered.

"Hey Dakota, Donte is out on Lalbert Road about four kilometers out. Can you drive the tow truck out there? Apparently, there is a guy in a Valiant that broke down."

"Yeah, not a prob. I'll head out now," he said.

"Thanks, Kota," I replied as I ended the call. I wasn't worried about him leaving the shop; Atticus was still working on a few services that we had to get done and Alena would be still in the office.

I sent a text back to Donte that Dakota was on his way. As soon as I got a thumbs-up, I slipped my phone back into my pocket and prepared for the next onslaught of pain that Burgess was about to subject me with.

Valiant. Damn, I loved old cars. I couldn't wait to get my hands on it. There was just something special about working on the old classics. So much better than the new stuff.

Chapter Five

P^{itt}

Donte came jogging back down the road towards me. The Valium had started to kick in, and I could feel the fogginess the was creeping over my mind. My shakes had begun to ease, and I breathed more calmly.

"Hey Pitt, you alright?" Donte asked.

I smiled lazily and nodded my head. "My meds have started to work. Thank you for not thinking I was a completely crazy person."

Donte chuckled and shook his head. "No bother. I have plenty of experience with people who struggle with anxiety. So, I just spoke to my boss, Obsidian; he is sending Dakota, another mechanic, out with the tow truck. You can either travel with him in the tow truck or on the back of the bike with me, and we can take you into town."

I winced as I thought about the cost. I had planned on sleeping in Valerie to not have to pay for motels.

"How much are motels?" I asked.

Donte shrugged his shoulders. "I don't know for sure. Listen, are you broke?"

I sighed. "No, probably more stupid. I wanted to overcome my anxiety and step out of my comfort zone, so I thought the best way to do it was to go on a road trip. I was going to sleep in Valerie and then work in random towns to save some money to pay for fuel and stuff."

Donte nodded his head. "I take it you didn't have your car serviced before you left?"

I shook my head. "No. I had enough money to either service the car or travel for a few days. Now that Valerie has bit the dust, I'll have to use that money to get her fixed."

Donte bit into his bottom lip. "I'm with an MC, the Devil's Advocates. They are a mercenary group, not one of the bad MCs. Anyway, I know that Anghus, the president has loads of houses and apartments available on our compounds. I'm sure he wouldn't mind you staying in one. It wouldn't cost you anything other than a little help around the compound. I can ask him when I get into town if you want."

I nodded my head. "Thanks, Donte. I don't want to be a bother. I mean, I could just ring my Dad; I'm from Melbourne, so I haven't come very far, and I know that Dad would come and get me and take me home."

Donte shrugged. "If that is what you would rather do, then sure thing. But you wouldn't be a bother. And see it as part of the adventure. We have loads of omegas rescued from breeding facilities; they understand anxiety like yours. Some omegas have severe agoraphobia and can't even leave their home. That's why we are all understanding when it comes to mental illness. We have a psychologist who works out of the compound if you want to speak to someone."

"But I'm a complete stranger; why would you all do that for me?" I asked.

Donte shrugged his shoulders. "It's what they do. They accepted me even when I was a complete asshole to Anghus's mate's brother."

"I'll think about it and let you know once I'm back in town."

Donte nodded. "Sure thing. If you need to meet with Anghus first, I know he would be happy to meet with you. They really are awesome people. Anghus is terrifying to look at because he is like a million feet tall and a gargoyle alpha. But he is really just a big teddy bear."

I grinned. "You live out there?"

Donte smiled and nodded his head. "Yep, me and my mate, Savannah. Her brother is mated to my boss's brother Asher. Weirdly we are all like connected."

"One big family," I said, feeling the sleepiness of the Valium washing over me.

Donte chuckled. "Yep. Rest, I can see the meds taking you away to snooze town. Dakota will be here in a minute, and we will get you into Lalbert."

"Thanks," I muttered.

When I blinked my eyes open again, it was Donte shaking me and another man looking at me with a smile.

"Hey there," the other man said with a grin; from his scent, I could tell he was fae. That and the mischief in his eyes.

"Hi, sorry, I didn't mean to sleep," I said.

"Not a worry. I need you to hop out of the car, though, so I can hook her up to the tow truck," the man said. "I'm Dakota, by the way."

"Nice to meet you, Dakota; I'm Pitt."

Dakota smiled, and I climbed out of the driver's seat and watched as he and Donte started hooking Valerie to the tow truck. Once she was on the truck's bed, Donte returned to me.

"Do you want to go in the tow truck or on the back of the bike?"

I glanced between him and the tow truck. My logical brain said to go in the tow truck, but my sense of adventure was begging me to go on the bike. I knew I'd kick myself later if I didn't step out of my comfort zone. Especially if I had to ring Dad to come and pick me up.

"I'll come on the bike," I said.

Donte grinned and nodded his head. "Come on. I'll grab you a helmet."

As soon as I had the helmet strapped on and was safely on the back of the bike, Donte revved the engine to life, and we took off. My arms and thighs squeezed tight to Donte, but the feeling of freedom was exhilarating.

Chapter Six

Obsidian

"You've got sauce on your chin, you slob," Iver giggled as we sat opposite each other at Tabbies, gorging on hamburgers.

I chuckled and reached out for a napkin to wipe my chin. "Did I get it?"

Iver snorted and shook his head. He took the napkin out of my hand and wiped my face. "There."

"Thanks, man," I said as I bit into my burger again.

"You need an omega to take care of you," Tabby said as she refilled mine and Iver's sodas.

"I wish," I mumbled with my mouth full.

"You'll find someone one day," Tabby replied.

"Sooner than he realizes," Iver responded.

I looked at my nephew with wide eyes. "Yeah?"

Iver nodded his head and smiled. "But that's all I'm gonna say."

I nodded. It was enough. I couldn't wait to meet a mate. If Iver said there would be one coming to me soon, that was enough for me. I was prepared to wait if there was someone to wait for.

Once we finished our burgers, I leaned back in the chair and rubbed my belly. "That hit the spot."

"Got room for dessert?" Tabby asked.

I shook my head. "Not for me, but the young fella might."

Tabby glanced at Iver, who waved his hand and shook his head. "No, I couldn't possibly eat anything else."

"What? I thought you were a growing boy?" Tabby laughed.

Iver giggled and nodded his head. "I am, but that burger was huge."

Tabby grinned. "I hope you enjoyed it."

"You outdid yourself, Tabby," I said. "It was beautiful."

Tabby leaned down and pressed a kiss to the top of my head. "I can always count on the Rigby's to make my day."

"You ready to get home and show your parents your new tattoo?" I asked.

Iver grinned and nodded his head; sliding out of the booth, he stood and waited for me to pay our tab and then follow me out to the car. We turned the music up loud and were wailing as I pulled into the compound. I pulled up to the main house and climbed out of the car.

"Hey, we are home," I called out as I opened the door to the main house.

"Alright, show us your work," Joachim said to Iver as he came out of the kitchen.

Iver stripped out of his shirt and turned his back to show his father. Joachim grinned. "Dad is going to love that," he said. Sloane had outdone herself on Iver's kraken. "What did you get?"

I stripped out of my shirt and turned my back. I'd added my latest niece to my back. Whisper's face shone beside her brother, Nasuth's.

"I love it," Joachim said. "If I was brave enough to get a tattoo, I'd love to do something for the kids."

"You should ask Burgess; he is a gentle tattooist."

Iver bust out a laugh. "That's not what you were saying when he was tattooing you. I believe there were a bunch of four-letter words."

I chuckled. "You said you wouldn't tell."

Iver laughed and shook his head. "I said I wouldn't tell Dad. Papa knows how much you swear."

I glanced over at Joachim, who nodded his head. "Did you want to join us for dinner? Lynx and Israel have the smoker going, and we were going to have a cookout."

I shook my head. "Normally I would, but I got a car towed in today, and I want to check it out before we shut up for the night. Donte said it'd blown a head gasket and a water valve, so I wanted to order new parts before they shut for the weekend."

Joachim shook his head. "I have no idea what they are. But no worries."

I chuckled and leaned forward, pressing a kiss to my brother in laws cheek before kissing Iver.

"See ya, buddy. Let me know what your old man thinks of your tattoo," I said.

Iver grinned and nodded his head. "I will. See ya, Uncle Sid."

I waved goodbye and walked out the door and down to my car. I spotted Donte coming into the compound with someone on the back of his bike. I waved my hand and brought my car to life as I pulled out and headed back into the shop to check out the Valiant that had been towed in.

Chapter Seven

P^{itt}

The bike ride to Obsidian Mechanics was enthralling. Donte helped me to climb off the bike, and when I stood on the ground it felt like the vibrations were still working through my legs. I'd never felt anything so freeing in my life.

Donte chuckled. "You'll get used to it," he said as I pat my legs.

Dakota had backed the tow truck into the garage and pulled Valerie off the back of the truck when another man slipped out from under a car.

"Oh wow, she's an original," he gushed. I felt myself grow with pride. It was great being around others that loved Valerie as much as I did. "She yours?"

I nodded my head. "Valerie."

The man smiled, showing his fangs, telling me he was a vampire. "I'm Atticus. I was busy with a service when Dakota left; what's happened to Valerie?"

I shrugged my shoulders. "As much as I love cars, I don't know much about them, I'm afraid."

Atticus smiled and shook his head. "Don't worry about it."

"Looks like a blown head gasket and water valve," Donte said.

Atticus nodded his head. "Hopefully, we can get the parts. Are you planning on staying in Lalbert for a while?"

I sighed and shrugged again. "I hadn't even planned on stopping for more than some lunch when Valerie broke down. Donte offered me to stay out at the Devil's Advocates compound, but I didn't want to be a burden on anyone."

Atticus shook his head. "Shit, no, you wouldn't be a burden out there. I guarantee they would love to have you."

I bit into my lip and nodded my head. If it wasn't for the valium still in my system, I knew my anxiety would be fighting to take over. I could feel my hands beginning to shake. Donte moved to stand next to me, and I could feel the warmth of his body on my arm. It seemed to have an instant calming effect which was strange.

"How much do you think it will cost to fix Valerie?" I asked.

Atticus shrugged his shoulders. "Hard to say. She's a classic, which means parts can be tricky to get a hold of. However, in saying that, Obsidian loves his classic cars, so he will probably know where to pick up the parts we need to fix it. But you are looking probably around a grand."

I sighed out a breath. It was less than I expected, but it would leave me with nothing if they didn't find anything else wrong with Valerie. My only other choice was to ring my Dad and have him come get me and start my trip at another time. I really didn't want to do that. As anxious as I was, I didn't want to back away from this. I tried to be strong and keep fighting.

"Are there many jobs going in this area?" I asked.

Donte nodded his head. "Yep. There are a few restaurants, cafes, a pub, and even a kink club."

My eyes widened, and my mouth dropped open. "I thought this was a little town."

"It's more like a little city. Compared to Melbourne, it's a town, but we have pretty much everything we need here," Atticus explained.

"Well, at least I could get some work. I can gather some more money to continue my trip," I said.

"Sure, you can. Where are you going to stay, at least for tonight?" Donte asked.

I glanced over at him and scratched my chin. "Are you sure Anghus won't mind?"

"I'm positive, but I'll ring him now, and you can hear for yourself."

I nodded my head. I felt much more comfortable knowing that the Devil's Advocate's president would be alright with having a stranger stay at their compound. But if he wasn't, I would find a motel. If I was really careful with money and found a job quickly, I could afford to stay in a motel for a few days and then look at perhaps even sharing a house if someone wanted a border.

"Hey, Donte, what's up?" A man's voice came through Donte's phone.

"Anghus. I have a guy here; his name is Pitt. He has found himself stranded in Lalbert. His car broke down, but he doesn't have a whole lot of cash to be able to get a motel as well as fix his car. Is it alright if we put him up for a bit?"

"Yeah, man, of course. If you think he is a good guy, then I trust your opinion," Anghus said.

"He is a shifter and omega. From what I can tell, he is good, doesn't set off my powers," Donte answered as he looked me up and down.

I didn't even know what that meant, but if it meant I could stay somewhere, then that suited me.

"Good enough for me, man. Bring him by the main house first, and we will sort out a place for him."

"Thanks, Anghus; see you in about an hour or so," Donte said before ending the call. "There you go; it's all good."

I smiled. "What do you mean by your powers weren't set off?"

Donte grinned. "One thing about the Devil's Advocates, they are a very spiritual people. They believe in the old gods and the powers that supernaturals were given. My power is that I can tell when someone is lying."

My eyes widened, and my mouth dropped open. "Seriously?"

"Yep, tell me two truths and a lie, and I'll show you."

I hummed as I thought about what I could tell him. "Okay. I was homeschooled, worked in a restaurant, and my favorite color is purple."

Donte smiled. "That's an easy one. Your favorite color isn't purple. I'm betting it's white."

My eyes widened again. "Yeah, that was right. Holy shit. So, all supernaturals have powers like that?"

"Sure, they do. They all have different powers. Anghus is the one to ask about it; he knows a lot more than me. I'm still learning."

"Wow, I think I'd like to learn too. I wonder what my powers would be, I always just thought I was a shifter, nothing special."

Donte grinned. "You'll get a chance to when we go out to the compound. So, why don't you grab what you need, and then we can head out."

I nodded my head and went to my car, popping the trunk. I pulled out my backpack with my phone charger, medications, and a couple of changes of clothes. I could get the rest from my car later if I needed them. I knew I should be terrified heading back to the Devil's Advocates compound, but something in me was calm. It was like I knew I was doing the right thing. Maybe this was my supernatural power.

Chapter Eight

Obsidian

After dropping Iver home, I went back to the shop. The best part about owning Papa's old mechanic shop was the apartment above it. I never had far to go home. I loved what I did. I'd always loved cars. If I could have skipped school to work on vehicles with Papa, I would have. But Mama and Papa had insisted I at least finish high school before I take on an apprenticeship. Out of all my brothers, I think I was the only one Papa knew would follow in his footsteps.

The minute I had that last day of school, I was ready. Papa taught me everything he knew. Then when he decided to retire, he gave me the shop as a gift. He told me the only thing he wanted was for me to rename it to make it mine. I was never very creative, hence the name Obsidian Mechanics. It didn't matter; I built up my clientele and took over what Papa left me. Soon, it went from just me and Atticus working to a slew of employees.

I walked into the office where Alena was packing up for the evening. "Hey, you off?" I asked.

Alena looked up and grinned before nodding her head. "Yep. I have a wild weekend of reading ahead."

I cackled and waved goodbye as she strutted out of the office and towards her motorbike. Alena was the most complexed person I'd ever met. It was almost like she had two completely different people living inside her. Some might have thought that perhaps she did as a trans woman. But that wasn't what I meant. Alena rode a big Fat Boy Harley. She dressed in leather and looked like she could easily give any dominatrix a run for their money. But then she loved nothing more than staying home, reading, and not talking to anyone for an entire weekend. I loved her no matter who she was. I was lucky to have her working for me.

We'd had a few customers who'd left after I employed Alena because of the fact that she was transgendered. I didn't care that they left. I didn't want bigots for clients anyway. Alena was great at her job, she greeted everyone with a friendly smile and treated them all like VIPs and that was what I loved about having her as an employee. I didn't care what genitalia she had or didn't have, that wasn't my business. My business was fixing cars and making sure that my clients were happy with my work.

Actually, I was lucky to have all my staff. Atticus had been with me the longest; he'd also been one of Papa's employees. If I'm correct, I think he even may have worked for my grandfather before Papa took over the business. Rigby Motors had been in the family since my Grandpa started it when he was seventeen. I didn't know a whole lot about Grandpa's early years, but I do know that he grew up rough. His family kicked him out of the house when he was only fifteen years old, and then he found himself in Lalbert. Somehow, he'd stumbled on some money and started Rigby Motors. Papa sometimes thinks that Rigby wasn't even Grandpa's real last name, but it was a name he took because he wasn't proud of where he came from.

Bacchus had done some research into the Rigby family name; apparently, there isn't a whole lot known. Well, none that he talked about. When I was about four years old, something happened, and Grandpa was killed. Papa took over the shop and continued running it like his Papa did. Grandpa was mated to my Granddad, but once Grandpa died, it didn't take long, and Grandpa followed him to the other side. Grandad had been a builder in Lalbert and was a lot more well known. His family was very spiritual and from what I knew they'd come from Scotland as bear shifters. They'd followed the power of the supernatural to Lalbert. Grandad often talked about how Lalbert was built on the fae lines and that meant there was more power and healing in this little town than in any other place he'd seen.

Mama told me it was the heartbreak that killed Granddad. I often wondered if something happened to Papa or Mama and whether the other would die shortly afterward. I couldn't imagine the hurt it would cause to lose a mate. Especially one that you are fated to, like Mama and Papa.

Walking into the workshop, I glanced at the new car sitting with its bonnet up. Sucking in a deep breath, I shook my head before the cloud of longing fell over me. It filled me with joy, but at the same time, I was impatient. I had to keep reminding myself that Iver said my mate would come sooner than I expected.

Atticus was leaned over the engine of the beautiful but beat to hell Valiant with his tools.

"She's a beauty," I said as I walked up beside the vampire.

"She sure is. Valerie, her name is apparently," Atticus said with a chuckle. "The poor guy that owns her was a bit of a wreck. Donte told me he was in complete meltdown when he first spotted him. The kid's name is Pitt. Has to take Valium and stuff just to get through a panic attack."

"Shit," I said with a shake of my head. "That must be awful. Where was he from?"

"Melbourne. From what Donte told me, he was trying to step out of his comfort zone by traveling around Australia. But the problem was he only had enough money to either travel or get Valerie serviced. He chose to travel."

I winced. "Poor Valerie. Well, we will make her happy again. What do you reckon?"

Atticus nodded his head. "Yeah, she is going to need a whole new engine, I think," he said with a wince.

"Oh no," I groaned.

"Yeah, I don't know how to break it to the kid. But there is much more wrong here than just a head gasket and water valve. This is the original motor, and I'm surprised she has lasted this long."

I sighed. "And he won't have the money to buy a new engine, I'm betting."

Atticus nodded his head. "He has gone back to the Devil's Advocates for tonight, and he was talking about getting work to pay for his trip, but I'm not sure if he will be able to get up enough cash fast enough to get her back on the road."

"I'll talk to him on Monday and explain the problem. Over the weekend, I'll do some research; maybe I can find a reconditioned motor that we can grab cheap, which will help keep costs down. Otherwise, we will have to work something out. If he plans to stick around Lalbert for a while, maybe I can get him to work here to pay off the work. Might even be able to teach him how to look after his own car."

Atticus chuckled. "I don't know that he would be any good working in a customer service role, so he would probably be better suited in the shop."

I nodded my head. I knew a little bit about anxiety. I couldn't imagine being that scared of everything. I saw the omegas the Devil's Advocates took on and how frightened they were. Not to mention March, when Asher first introduced us, was as timid as they came. But I didn't know someone that needed Valium just to be able to survive in the world. That was an awful thought.

"Alright, I'm going to head up for the night. I need a shower, and then I think some time in front of the television," I said with a yawn.

"No worries, I'm just gonna lock up here, and then I'll join you," Atticus replied.

Atticus and I had decided to share the apartment above the shop, seeing as it had three bedrooms. Grandpa and Grandad had lived there with Papa. It wasn't until Papa met Mama that he moved out and bought the home we were all raised in. Not that seven kids would have fit in the apartment. But for Atticus and me, it worked. And I liked having someone to live with; it kept the loneliness at bay.

Chapter Nine

P^{itt} I spent the weekend getting to know many of the members of the Devil's Advocates. There wasn't a single person that I met that I didn't like. Some were more serious than others, and some were slightly dubious of a stranger in the compound, but I still felt welcomed.

"We pretty much have everything we need here. This is the school. All the kids living in the compound are given a choice to either attend public school in Lalbert or do a version of home education here," Joachim said as they walked through the compound.

"That is amazing. Who teaches the kids?" I asked.

"We have a couple of teachers. But Amos, who is mated to Jasper, my brother-in-law, is a special education teacher. We also have Aila, Elmer, Carol, and Leona, who teach based on age. Elmer and Carol teach the older kids that would be high school age, while Aila and Leona teach the younger kids. Then Amos helps out in the younger kids group because he is currently working with Daffodil, Jasper and Amos's daughter, and Amos's nephew Negus. Daffodil has Down Syndrome, while Negus has Dyslexia."

"Wow, that is amazing that you even have catered for special needs kids," I said in astonishment. The more I learned about the Devil's Advocates, the more I liked them.

Joachim nodded his head. "We hadn't until Jasper got custody of Daffodil a couple of years ago. We hadn't really had a need, but when we hired Amos, we also found out that Jasper and Amos were fated, mates."

My eyes widened. "This is so awesome. The way fate has worked for you all."

"Do you come from a family that celebrates being supernatural?"

I shrugged my shoulders. "Yeah. Dad and Papa have always been very proud of their supernatural roots and heritage. But my brothers and sister were all sent to a mixed school, so we didn't tend to learn a lot about what was involved in being supernatural. I didn't even know that supernaturals could have other powers beyond the ordinary. Still, Donte said that you all learn all about your powers."

Joachim grinned and nodded his head. We were walking toward the back of the property, where a vast forest sat, and I could see a massive garden filled with vegetables. The more time I spent here, I almost wished I didn't have to leave. I mean, I was going to have to stay in Lalbert for a while to afford to make some more money before I could travel again, but I didn't want to leave this compound. It had everything.

"Yes, it's true. I didn't know it either. But I was raised in a breeding facility, so I didn't know much. If it hadn't been for Anghus's father, I possibly wouldn't have even known how to read."

I frowned and shook my head. "His father?"

Joachim chuckled and nodded. "It's a long story. But Anghus's father, Jantzen, is also the stepson of Ettore, a Nephilim and basically our arch-nemesis. Ettore owned the breeding facility where I was raised. I was intended for breeding because I was an omega. But I hadn't gone into heat. As it turned out, I didn't go into heat because I hadn't met my mates. But anyway, Jantzen was also raised basically in the breeding facility. Still, instead of an omega, he is an alpha dragon shifter sent by Ettore to other breeding facilities to impregnate their omegas. However, one of the omegas, Anghus's mother, Gwen, was his fated mate. He tried to take Gwen out of the breeding facility but was stopped by Ettore. So, in the end, the AJE authority shut down the breeding facilities that Gwen was in and then later on, the did the same to the one that I was in and broke apart Morpheus."

"Holy shit," I said with wide eyes. "What happened to Ettore?"

"He managed to get away. Ever since, the AJE authority, the Devil's Advocates, and the Onyx Rebels have been hunting him to bring him to justice. But there is a prophecy that Ettore will create a war, and the children of this generation will rise up with the power of the gods to end him.”

"And you believe the prophecy?"

Joachim nodded his head. "Yep. Every word of it."

"How do you know it's true?" I asked.

"We are seeing children born that are not only the rarest supernatural species but have powers like we've never seen before."

I shook my head in shock. "Like what?"

"Well, my son, Iver, is cthulu. He talks directly to the creator and can bring messages. We are learning more about his power every day. But he can also connect with a baby's spirit while growing in the womb. He can tell you the future, pretty much everything. Then there is Daffodil. She might be a dragonfly shifter, but she has a constant presence of the ancestors following her around. They aren't the only two. We have nuckalavee, karkadann, pixcu, bi'an, kumiho, and valkyrie, just to mention a few."

"Holy shit," I whispered. "And they all have powers?'

Joachim nodded his head. "Yeah, they are completely awe-inspiring to watch."

"I haven't even heard of some of those you mentioned," I admitted.

Joachim chuckled. "Neither had we. And looking at them, you'd never know what they are. Their scent is so different from anyone we have ever met. In fact, in cases like Lynx's two sons, Forrest and River, they are nuckalavee. According to Arcadia, the record keeper for supernaturals, the nuckalavee had been thought to be extinct for thousands of years."

"Oh my god. And they came back. Well, now I can see why you believe in the prophecy; it's pretty hard to deny that something big will happen when you look at what is happening around you."

Joachim smiled and nodded his head. "This is our vegetable garden. We grow as much of our food as possible. With the number of omegas coming to live here, we try to cut costs. That way, no one is forced to work, and those that need to heal can heal."

"I was going to ask what you all did to make money. I mean, most MCs are slinging drugs or shifting weapons. But you don't seem to be doing anything like that."

Joachim nodded again. "Yep. So, Anghus is the president of the Devil's Advocates. But it was started by a man named Declan. Morpheus sadly killed him, and we believe it was by Ettore's command. When he died, Lynx, one of the founding members, inherited all of Declan's money, so he started setting up a compound. Then they found out this place, owned by Declan's parents, had been left to Declan, but no one had been able to find him. When Lynx got in contact with a lawyer, that's how he found out. So, we set up here. Lynx uses the money he inherited to put back into the MC, and the members who work with the AJE authority get paid from them also. Plus, some of the omegas like to be able to work outside of the compound and have jobs in Lalbert. Not to mention that the MC often gets paid for mercenary jobs they take on."

"Sounds like you all have it sorted out," I said.

Joachim chuckled. "We do. But there are always so many people that we still have yet to rescue."

"There are still breeding facilities?" I asked. I'd heard about the AJE authority shutting down Morpheus. But I thought they'd closed all of the facilities.

"Yeah, there are. Sadly, with Ettore still free, he has set up more facilities. The breeding facilities will likely remain until we can shut him down. We just recently shut one down in Siberia. The omegas were all brought here to live. Most of them were already pregnant. And as young as fourteen."

My eyes widened, and I gasped as I shook my head. "That makes me sick," I growled.

"Me too. It's why we do what we do."

"I can appreciate that. I wish there was a way I could help."

"There is. Become a member of the Devil's Advocates."

I frowned. "But don't I need a motorbike for that?"

Joachim grinned and shook his head. "Na. Lots of members don't have bikes. Many do because they enjoy riding, but many omegas don't ride."

I nodded my head. Since coming to the Devil's Advocate compound, I couldn't ignore the fact that I hadn't had to rely on the Valium. I hadn't had a single anxiety attack. I wasn't sure if that was because I felt safe and comfortable here or if it was some kind of power they had.

"I will think about it," I promised.

"No pressure. We will help you regardless. Even if it is just to give you a place to stay while you look for somewhere more permanent or move on with your travels."

I smiled at Joachim and nodded my head. That was the other thing I liked about them. They didn't judge. They let me be me. The thought of leaving this place was going to be a tricky one. I wasn't sure that I wanted to leave. But I also didn't want to be a burden.

Chapter Ten

O bsidian

I'd spent the weekend chasing up a new engine for Valerie. I'd spoken with Bacchus, who told me Pitt was fitting in well at the Devil's Advocates compound but seemed nervous about money. After looking at Valerie Saturday morning I realized that Atticus was right. We could replace the parts that had broken, but it wouldn't take long before the whole engine needed replacing.

Don't called me and told me how Pitt struggles badly with anxiety. Atticus had said he needed Valium when the pressure was terrible, so I wanted to try and keep the costs down as low as possible. Some might say I was a sucker, but I couldn't help it. My heart always tore for people when they were in need, and after hearing Atticus, Bacchus and Donte tell me about Pitt's anxiety, my heart wanted to reach out and make it alright for him.

On Monday, I'd finally managed to track down an engine and went into the shop with plans to pull out the old motor, so we just had to place in the new one and connect it all up. I'd been able to swing a good deal on the reconditioned motor from Melbourne. One of the classic car mechanics I was friends with, Randon, hooked me up with an engine perfect for Valerie. It was being couriered up and should be ready for Wednesday.

I plucked my phone from my pocket as I reached the shop and scrolled until I found Anghus's number. I knew that Bacchus would be at work, and Donte was already at the shop.

"Hey, Sid, what's up?" Anghus asked.

"I didn't have a number for Pitt, but I just wanted to let him know I've found a new engine for his car. Could you please send him the message?"

"Sure can. Any idea on how much it's going to cost him. Knowing a price might let his anxiety ease a little."

"Yeah, that's cool. Don't tell him, but I will not charge for labor. The cost will be fifteen hundred."

"That's great; thanks for that, Obsidian. If you want the money for the labor, just write up an invoice, and I'll make sure I pay."

"Na man, it's okay. I'm the lucky one that gets to work on Valerie. She's a beauty," I replied.

Anghus chuckled before saying his goodbyes. I walked over to the car where Atticus and Donte were busy pulling the engine out of Valerie.

"I've got an engine coming for Wednesday," I said.

"Awesome. That will take a load off, Pitt, I reckon." Donte said.

"He was apprehensive about it?" I asked.

Donte sighed and nodded his head. "Yeah. I got the feeling his parents were expecting him to fail. From what he has said over the weekend, he was pretty much a shut-in. His anxiety caused him a lot of agoraphobia, so he often couldn't even step outside the house. He'd been working with his therapist to overcome the problems. This was his first time away from his parents, and he wanted to succeed."

I nodded my head. "So, his family decent people?"

Donte nodded. "Sounds that way. He rang them every day but hadn't told them about the car. He said his Dad would come to Lalbert to pick him up, and he didn't want that. He wants to prove to himself that he can do it independently."

"That's understandable," I said. It was why I'd chosen to live above the shop. I wanted to constantly show myself that I didn't need Mama and Papa. Of course, that didn't change my love for them. I wanted them constantly in my life, but I wanted to be independent.

I swung open the driver's side door to have a look inside. Suddenly the most erotic scent surrounded me, causing me to groan. My cock instantly hardened, and my eyes rolled as the scent enveloped me in loving arms.

"Holy shit, what is that?" I groaned.

"What?" Atticus asked.

"Can't you smell that?"

Atticus frowned and stepped into the car's door, shaking his head. "Nope. I can't smell anything other than the old car."

I shook my head. "That's not it. I can't explain the smell. But it's fresh and smells like whiskey and ice."

Atticus frowned and shook his head. "No, I definitely can't smell that."

I palmed my cock, adjusting it in my pants. It was throbbing hard. My panther was purring loudly and pushing close to the surface in an attempt to encourage me to roll around the back seat of the car.

"What is it?" I whispered. "I've never been affected by something like this. The scent is making me so horny I could cum just by inhaling. My panther is going wild, and I want to fuck into the back seat and leave my scent everywhere."

Atticus's eyes widened, and he gasped. "Wait. I think I know what is going on."

"What?"

"You've just found your mate."

My eyes widened, and I gasped. "Are you serious?"

Atticus nodded his head and smiled. "You are scenting something that I can't smell. You are horny, and you want to fuck and leave your scent behind to mingle with the one you can smell. Pitt is your mate."

"Holy shit," I said with shock. "I want a mate, but now I'm scared. He doesn't want to stay in Lalbert. He wants to travel. What if that means he doesn't want me?"

Atticus shrugged his shoulders. "I suggest you go and find out. He might surprise you. From what Donte said, he is happy at the compound. Maybe he is getting a pull to set down roots."

"I guess. At least in Lalbert, he would still be close to his family," I mused.

Atticus nodded his head. "And you can take a holiday, you know, and travel."

I chuckled and shrugged my shoulders. "I guess. But there isn't much point in making these plans until I know he wants me."

"I think you should warn Anghus before you go out there. Let Anghus talk to Pitt. If it's not something he wants, you don't want to send him into heat if he is planning on leaving."

I nodded my head. "That's what I'll do."

I pulled my phone out of my pocket and scanned through to Anghus's number again. Anghus answered with a chuckle. "Did you forget something?"

"Sort of. Anghus, I've just found my mate. He is Pitt," I said with a shock that out of all the places that Pitt could break down, it was here in Lalbert, and it was Donte that happened upon him on the side of the road.

"Oh wow, that is awesome, man. Congratulations."

"I'm stuck, though. I don't know if Pitt wants me. I was hoping that maybe you could ask if he would want a mate. I don't want to send him into heat if he doesn't want me."

"Of course. I can do that. Give me an hour, and I'll ring you back to let you know."

"Thank you, Anghus and give that boy of yours a big hug from Uncle Sid; he told me on Friday that my mate was closer than I expected."

Anghus chuckled again. "Trust my kid."

I smiled. I loved that Iver had told me. I just hoped that Pitt wanted me in return.

Chapter Eleven

Pitt

I was helping Trudy in the garden mid-Monday morning when I saw Anghus and Joachim walking hand in hand. I smiled up at them. To look at Anghus, you would easily assume he was an angry, giant gargoyle who would rip you to pieces. And in a way, I guess that was true. I mean, I imagine if you hurt his mates or children, he would indeed be that gargoyle. But the way he walked with Joachim was so gentle and the love on his face when he looked at either of his mates or children was all-encompassing.

"Pitt, just the man we were looking for," Joachim said with a grin as they reached where I'd been weeding.

"Hey there. What did you need?" I asked as I stood from the ground and wiped my dirty hands on my jeans.

"Well, I got a call from Obsidian today," Anghus said.

"Oh, awesome. Were they able to find an engine for my car?"

Anghus nodded his head. "Yep. It should be here on Wednesday, and then they said you should have your car back and ready by Monday. But there is something else you need to know."

I frowned and felt my anxiety begin to kick into overdrive. "Wwwwwhat is it?" I asked, stumbling over my words.

Joachim reached out a hand and touched my arm lightly. "It's nothing to get anxious about. There is nothing wrong," he assured me with a warm smile.

I nodded and bit my cheek as I breathed slowly out of my nose, trying to expel the anxiety threatening to take over.

"Have you ever thought about your fated mate?" Anghus began.

I shook my head. "No. Not really. I figured I might have a mate out there and I'd meet them one day, but that's as far as I ever got. Why?"

Anghus and Joachim shared a look. Joachim smiled and turned back to me. "When Obsidian rang, he said he'd opened your car and could scent you. He believes that you might be his mate. He was prepared to come here but wasn't sure if you wanted a mate or if you still wanted to travel. So, he didn't want to come and potentially throw you into heat if you didn't want him."

I gasped, and my eyes widened. My mouth dropped open, and I shook my head. Even my anxiety didn't have time to go off due to the shock I was feeling.

"He is my mate?" I asked dumbly. I mean, they had just told me he was.

"I think so," Anghus replied. "But Obsidian comes from a family that is very proud about being supernatural. But they are also very conscious that not everyone wants to be mated or believes in fated mates. So, he didn't want to push anything on you. That's why he asked us to talk to you first. He is conscious of the fact that you had wanted to travel and that you aren't from Lalbert. But if you are mated to Obsidian, it puts a bit of a spanner in the works. Obsidian can't just pack up and leave to travel with you; his life is here in Lalbert. I know that he would be willing to move, but it's not something he could do easily."

I nodded my head. "I understand that. I wouldn't want to take him away from his family and friends anyway."

Anghus nodded. "Obsidian doesn't expect you to immediately give him an answer, but he probably won't come to see you unless you decide you want to mate with him. He also wouldn't want to take you away from your family and friends either."

"I appreciate that," I said. "I need to think about it. I had my heart set on traveling, but now I'm unsure what to do."

"Take all the time you need. You are welcome to stay here. It's been a pleasure getting to know you."

"Thank you Anghus, and Joachim. I've got a lot to think about. But I really do appreciate you both taking me as you have. Everyone has made me feel so welcome; it's like I found a family outside my family. I never expected to find that."

"That has to be just about the biggest compliment anyone has ever given us," Joachim said with a smile. "We have always strived to make people feel at home when they come here. So, knowing that you have felt like you are family makes my whole day."

I smiled again. "Do you mind if I go into the forest and shift for a while? I find I can think better that way."

Anghus grinned and nodded his head. "Go for it. Others may be out there, but they won't bother you."

"Thanks again," I said as I turned away and began to strip from my clothes. As soon as I was naked, I called my bear forward and felt my body begin to change. I blinked open my eyes and saw the world with the sharp crispness that only being altered ever gave.

I breathed in deeply and started a slow jog into the forest. I needed time to think. A mate. I couldn't believe it. Maybe there was something in fate. *Why else would I have broken down and happened to have been found by a mechanic that worked with Obsidian?*

But now I had a decision. *Did I stay here and make a life with my mate? Or did I leave and keep traveling and hope that one day, if I returned, fate hadn't turned her back on us.*

Chapter Twelve

O bsidian

I was pacing back and forth across the shop floor, waiting for Anghus to call me back with how Pitt reacted to the news that I was his mate. My stomach was a riot of turmoil as I thought of the potential that Pitt didn't want me. I knew it would be hard to face that rejection, but I would never force myself on someone. Especially someone who has already struggled with mental health problems.

My phone buzzed in my pocket, and I dived for it. "Anghus?" I answered without even looking at the screen.

My brother, Bacchus's voice, barked out a laugh on the other end. "Should I be worried that you are so excited to hear from my mate, little brother?"

I sighed. "No. I am waiting for him to call me back with a response from Pitt."

"Well, lucky then I'm calling you because Anghus got called into the AJE authority for some work, but he told me about his meeting with Pitt. Apparently, Pitt seemed to take the news alright but wanted to think about it over the next few days."

"Okay, that's fair," I replied even though my panther basically howled inside me. He wanted to go and get his mate. But I knew we had to be patient. If nothing else, Mama and Papa had taught us the importance of restraint and patience. "Do you think that he will want me?"

"I don't know, Sid. I'm sorry, I just don't know. Anghus and Joachim explained everything to him. They told Pitt the reason you hadn't come to find him yourself. He seemed happy but then said he needed to shift for a while and think about what he wanted to do. This is a big decision for him."

I sighed. "I know."

"It's not even just about mating. It's about upheaving his entire life and his plans. Anghus told him that you weren't in a position to drop everything and travel with him like he'd planned and that you would never expect to pull him away from his family."

"That's all true. But I'm not sure I want to leave my family either."

"Well, the plus side is that Pitt is from Melbourne, so you are only a few hours down the road if you decide to move. But don't go making any plans yet. Wait until you find out what Pitt actually wants. You know how much people hate it when their decisions are made for them. Even with Pitt's anxiety, I can't imagine he would be thrilled if you just assumed what he wanted."

"I understand. I don't want to do that. I want him to be equal."

"That's the way. Now, how much work have you managed to get done today?"

I chuckled. "Not much. I've constantly been thinking about Pitt."

"Thinking or worrying?"

"Worrying," I admitted.

"I'd invite you to the main house for dinner, but I think that might be a temptation too hard for you at the moment. Why don't you give Mama a call and go there for dinner?"

I sighed and nodded my head even though I knew that Bacchus wouldn't be able to see it.

"Yeah, maybe. I've got a few things I need to do, so I'll stick my head down and get working. I'm glad that Pitt didn't run for the hills when the mateship was mentioned to him."

"I guarantee he hasn't run for the hills; you've still got his car for one. But Iver mentioned to me this morning that he hopes Pitt will stay. I think the cheeky kid knows more about it but isn't willing to say anything."

"Iver is growing up so fast. Hard to believe that he will be eleven soon."

Bacchus sighed. "I know. It almost makes me want more."

"Joachim and Anghus would be up for that?"

"I know Anghus would be, but I don't know about Joachim. I have been hinting a little lately, but either Joachim hasn't picked up on my hints or is ignoring them."

I laughed. "Well, for the time being, you have plenty of nephews and nieces to dote on. Not to mention all the club members popping out babies, left, right and center."

"I love on every one of them too."

Bacchus was a real softy. It didn't matter that he was a big burly cop. Underneath it all, he was a tender-hearted person who melted at the sight of babies and animals.

Chapter Thirteen

P^{itt}

I spent the rest of the day shifting and playing in the creek at the bottom of the Devil's Advocates compound. I'd discovered a couple of others that were shifted, but for the most part, it was just me. It gave me a chance to think about everything. I had been so determined to travel around Australia and break free from my dependence on Dad and Papa. But now that I knew I had Obsidian as a mate, traveling didn't seem so important.

The only question I had was if I mated with Obsidian, would I be giving up one dependence to go to another? I wanted the chance to be my own person. To not be afraid the minute I walked out the door. I thought that's what I would have when I started traveling.

But when I thought about the Devil's Advocates compound, I'd felt that sense of freedom too. The people that lived here were all so understanding and welcoming. I hadn't needed my anxiety medication. In fact, the last time I'd even taken a dose of Valium was on the Friday that I broke down.

Even when I did start to panic and stutter, they gave me the space to calm down and lent me their strength. It wasn't a place I necessarily wanted to leave. I didn't know if that was because this compound was more like a family than living in any other community or if it was Lalbert as a whole. I knew that if Obsidian and I moved back to Melbourne, I would soon shrink away again.

The chances were that Obsidian would want to break things off with me because he wouldn't be able to stand that I didn't want to go outside. At least staying here, I was only a few hours from Dad and Papa. They could come to visit, or when my car was fixed, I could quickly go and see them.

I'd already been planning on staying somewhere to make money before moving on. Dad and Papa would welcome Obsidian, so I wasn't worried there. But I also felt that it was unfair to expect Obsidian to uproot his whole life to move to Melbourne for me. After all, I had already uprooted my life, which was my plan, until I landed here in Lalbert.

As I walked back into the apartment Anghus had let me stay in I continued to think about what I wanted. I knew that my bear wanted desperately to mate with Obsidian, there was no doubt coming from him. So, really the only thing that was holding me back from mating with Obsidian was whether I wanted to continue to travel or not. It was all down to me. *Could I be happy having not achieved my goal of traveling?*

I hummed and sat down on the couch before pulling my phone out. I scrolled through the contacts before finding my sister, Talia. She was always the one I turned to when I had a dilemma. I don't know how but she seemed to constantly help to sort my head out when it was muddled.

The phone rang as I waited for Talia to answer. "Pitt are you okay?" she asked.

"Yeah, I'm fine. Don't tell Dad or Papa, but my car broke down on Friday, the very first damned day."

"Oh shit, where are you?" she asked with concern.

"In a town called Lalbert, about three hours from Melbourne. Valerie is at the mechanics. They are getting her a new motor."

"Where have you been staying?" Talia knew I'd planned to sleep in Valerie to save on costs.

"I'm staying at the Devil's Advocates MC compound. Have you heard of them?"

"Hell yeah, haven't you? They were on the news for shutting down breeding facilities with the AJE authority."

"I must've missed that," I said with a shake of my head. "Anyway, the guy that found me stranded on the side of the road happened to be a mechanic and work for Obsidian Mechanics in Lalbert and was a member of the Devil's Advocates, so he set everything up for me, which was great. But there is one problem."

"What's that?"

"I found my mate. Well, not technically. I haven't actually met him yet."

"Then how do you know he is your mate?" Talia asked, sounding confused.

"Obsidian owns the mechanics that Valerie is at. He opened the car today and realized my scent. He rang Anghus, the president of the Devil's Advocates, who also happens to be mated to Obsidian's brother. Obsidian asked Anghus if I was interested in having a mate. Obsidian didn't want to put me into heat, so didn't want to meet me if I wasn't interested in mating."

"Shit, that is confusing. Okay, so you have a dilemma, I'm assuming."

"Yeah," I replied. "I don't know whether to keep traveling and come back one day and hope that the mating bond is still there. Or whether to stay in Lalbert and mate with Obsidian."

Talia hummed. "I can see the dilemma. What is your brain saying?"

"Hmm, to stay."

"And your gut?"

I chuckled. "To stay."

"Then, my lovely, you don't need my help. You just solved your own dilemma. Don't forget that you have years and years to travel and sometimes having a mate to travel with is more fun. Remember how much fun Nathan had when he'd gone with Christopher to Italy last year. He said it was much better going with Christopher and the kids than when he went alone."

"Yeah, I remember, and I think you're right. At least I would feel more comfortable with having a traveling partner. But does that mean I will become too dependent on Obsidian like I was on Dad and Papa?"

"Well, for one, you were never too dependent on Dad and Papa. That was your head telling you that. You always worked, sure, you had to be homeschooled, but you could study independently. You didn't need Dad or Papa to be constantly looking over your shoulder. I mean, hell, if you were too dependent on them, you would never have left home to travel in the first place. And secondly, your mate is supposed to be the other half of your soul. If you don't depend on them, you might as well remain single. If you have good communication, then it allows Obsidian to tell you if you are becoming too clingy."

I sighed. She was right as always.

"Thank you, Talia. This is why I love you."

Talia cackled. "I love you too, Pitt. Now go get that mate of yours."

Chapter Fourteen

O bsidian

I felt like I was walking around in a daze. Every time I went near Valerie, I was enveloped by Pitt's scent. My cock was like steel; I'd never jerked off so many times in all my life. I was starting to worry that I would rip the skin from my shaft if I kept going. I was glad that Bacchus had called me with an update on Pitt, but it meant I had to wait. And although my parents had instilled patience as a valuable quality in us, I wasn't very good at practicing it.

"You gonna work today?" Atticus asked with laughter as he walked past me towards Valerie. He pulled the engine out with just him and Stagger the day before. I'd been no help.

"Ha ha," I said as I rolled my eyes. "I haven't been that bad, have I?"

Atticus threw his head back and barked out a laugh. "No. You haven't. You have shown a lot more restraint than a lot would. I'm just teasing you."

I sighed and scrubbed my hands over my face and through my hair. "This is killing me. Every time I get close to Valerie, I get fucking hard, and all I can think about is Pitt, and I don't even know what he looks like."

"Well, wonder no more," Donte responded as he entered the shop door.

I turned and standing beside Donte was the most beautiful man I'd ever seen in my life. He was tall for an omega. His long blonde hair was almost white, and his brown eyes were big as he watched me. I could see that he was nervous and knew I had to approach him gently.

"Pitt," I said quietly.

My mate smiled gently and nodded his head. He fidgeted his hands in front of him. "Hi Obsidian."

"Fuck, you are beautiful," I said as he basically took my breath away.

Pitt's cheeks tinted with a blush, making him look even more beautiful. I wondered if his cheeks would tint like that when he was cumming.

"Ah, guys, maybe you should take this upstairs, hey?" Atticus suggested breaking through the dream-like state I found myself in.

I nodded my head. "Do you want to go upstairs to my apartment? I promise not to touch you unless you want me to. You can leave at any time."

Pitt smiled and nodded his head. "I want to go upstairs with you."

My chest puffed with pride. That was the first step. I hoped that meant that he wanted to mate with me. He still hadn't come close enough that he would be going into heat yet. But I knew once we were in the apartment, I would only have a short amount of time to talk to him before his heat took over.

"It's this way," I said and started to lead the way to the stairs that climbed to the apartment. The feeling of Pitt right behind me was so strong. His scent surrounded me. I wanted to drink him down. I wanted to climb inside him and never come down. I'd never experienced anything so heady in all my life. It was such a weird feeling.

I opened the door to the apartment and led Pitt into the living room. Pitt sat down on the couch, and I sat beside him.

"Can I assume you've decided to mate with me?" I asked.

Pitt blushed again and nodded his head. "Yeah. I'm a bit nervous, though."

I nodded. "I know that Donte told me you have bad anxiety. I don't want to pressure you. That's why I didn't come to you. I didn't want to be too much."

Pitt breathed in deeply and slowly let it go. "Thank you. I've never met such amazing people before. Everyone has been so understanding. I do have anxiety. It can be completely debilitating sometimes. But since being in Lalbert, I don't know what it is, but it seems to be less. I haven't had the same number of panic attacks."

I smiled. "Lalbert is a special place. Have you ever been here before?" Pitt shook his head. "There is more time to explain it all later. There is a lot of magic in this town and the earth itself seems to have a life of its own that calls for supernaturals. But Lalbert is built on magical fae lines. It's a place of healing and a place of power."

Pitt nodded his head and smiled. "I believe you. The more I got to know many of the Devil's Advocates and spent time in the compound, the more I could feel that magic."

"The compound is the epicenter. Did Anghus tell you that?"

Pitt shook his head.

"Where the fae lines cross, the compound is built right in the middle. Apparently, the history is that it was built there on purpose by the angel that first came to Lalbert and created the Nephilim's that lived here. I don't know how true that is, but that is the legend. And it's why the place is so powerful and healing. They say the creek that runs through the property has magic and heals."

Pitt's eyes widened, and he gasped. "I've been so drawn to that creek. I wonder if that's why?"

I shrugged my shoulders. "It's possible. I don't know for sure. But if you ask any of the inner crew of the Devil's Advocates, they will tell you that it can regrow limbs. I'm not sure it's that powerful, but I think it is magical."

Pitt sat back on the couch further and breathed out. He seemed to have relaxed more as we talked.

"I want to mate with you, Obsidian," he said, looking up at me and pegging me with the most severe stare.

I bit into my bottom lip and nodded my head. "I want that too."

Chapter Fifteen

Pitt

Nothing could have prepared me for how hot Obsidian was. I'd been so nervous when I told Donte that I wanted to meet Obsidian this morning, and he offered to take me with him. When I walked into the shop and heard Obsidian talking about me, my nerves became slightly more substantial. But as soon as he turned around and I saw him for the first time, I think I could have just about fainted from the blood loss to my head that went racing straight to my cock.

He was everything I could want and more. Admittedly I'd never been with a man before. I wasn't a virgin, but my only experience was with our neighbor, who wanted to lose her virginity and asked if I'd help her. It had been a fumbling mess, but it also made me realize that I was missing out on a lot when I just used my hand to cum.

Obsidian's dark hair and almost black eyes were so serious, but at the same time, I could see the mischief that lay beyond them. He seemed to give off the image that he was a joker, but I think beneath it all, he was so sensitive, and things hurt him terribly. His presence completely calmed me so I could voice what I wanted. I didn't know if it was this power that Joachim talked about or because Obsidian was my mate, but I felt no nerves once we were alone.

I wanted him. Obsidian smiled gently at me and nodded his head. I could feel my heat starting to come on, and I knew that we wouldn't have long before I was too delirious to make sound decisions. If we were going to do this, we needed to talk about it now.

"Can I kiss you?" I asked boldly. My cheeks heated with embarrassment at my forwardness.

"Fuck yes," Obsidian answered, making me giggle. I moved forward on the couch and watched as Obsidian leaned in.

We were so close that I could feel his breath fanning across my lips. I'd never wanted anything or anyone like I wanted Obsidian. Breathing in deeply, I made that final move and connected our lips. At first, I planted small pecks across his lips. But then I slipped my tongue along his bottom lip. Taking advantage of Obsidian's gasp, I pushed my tongue forward to slide against his.

Obsidian groaned and gently stroked up my arms. I could tell that he was trying his hardest to hold himself back. But I didn't want that. I wanted to be manhandled. I wanted to be fucked. I needed all of the power that Obsidian had to give me.

I broke the kiss long enough to stand before I straddled his lap. I ground down against Obsidian's crotch, where his hard cock felt huge in his jeans. Obsidian looked up at me with hooded lids and moaned. I leaned forward and kissed him with all the passion I had. Obsidian grasped hold of my hips as I ground into him over and over, delighting in the feeling of his cock pressing against mine, even with the constraints of our jeans between us.

"Fuck, Pitt, you're going to make me cum in my jeans if we keep going," Obsidian panted.

I chuckled. "Then I guess we better get out of them," I replied.

Obsidian's smile was broad as he nodded his head. "Let's move to the bedroom. I share this place with Atticus. We don't need him coming in."

I nodded my head and stood. My cheeks heated at the thought of being caught by one of Obsidian's workmates. Obsidian followed me and took my hand as he led me down a short hallway into a painted black bedroom. The bed was massive and the only piece of furniture in the room were two black drawers beside the bed. The bed was covered in black velvet.

"Your favorite color is black?" I asked with a wry grin.

Obsidian laughed. "Everything about me is black. My panther, my name, my car, and my bedroom. What's your favorite color?"

"White," I said with a laugh. "But I'm quickly favoring black too."

Obsidian smiled and reached his hands to my shoulders. He skimmed his hands down over my arms before going for the hem of my shirt. He slipped my shirt up overhead and dropped it to the floor before working on undoing my jeans and letting them fall to my ankles. I kicked my shoes off and stepped out of my jeans as I reached for Obsidian's shirt and pulled it from his body, followed by his pants.

Once we were standing in our underwear, I took all of him in. If he hadn't told me he was a panther shifter, I would have quickly worked it out. He had a sleekness; he was slender but muscular at the same time. He was tall, and his muscles came from being a shifter and working hard. I stroked my fingers lightly down over his chest. Slick filled my boxers, and a wet patch was forming on the front of my underwear with precum.

"I need you," I whispered.

"You've got me," Obsidian answered as he leaned forward, pressed his lips against mine again, and pushed his tongue between my teeth.

Chapter Sixteen

Obsidian

I slipped down Pitt's boxers and groaned as his weeping cock bounced between us. Lowering to my knees, I opened my mouth and sucked him to the back of my throat. Pitt groaned and thrust his fingers through my hair. His scent was almost overpowering with how erotic it was. Fuck I've never wanted anyone like I did with Pitt. I continued to suck him up and down, delighting in the flavor of his precum on my tongue.

I fondled his balls in one hand while I moved the other around to his ass, sliding my fingers through his crack to find his hole leaking a steady stream of slick. Sliding my fingers up inside Pitt, I smiled around his cock at the intake of his sharp breath when I hit his prostate.

"Oh gods, Obsidian, that's going to make me cum," he purred.

I moaned around his cock and continued to press on his prostate. I wanted to make him cum so much that he couldn't possibly cum again. Pitt's fingers tightened in my hair as he began to thrust deeper into my throat. I felt his cock swell before he let out a long moan, and shots of cum sprayed against my tongue. I groaned as I drank down the salty seed.

I led Pitt to my bed and laid him on the blanket. Lifting my face from his dick, I looked up at my mate, watching me with hooded lids. I slowly stood and pulled my boxers down, stepping out of them.

Pitt lay on his back and lifted his legs automatically, opening himself up to me. The scent of his arousal was heady. I clasped Pitt's ankles as I lined myself up with his hole throbbing with need. His cock had remained hard, and from the glazed look in his eye, I knew he was in full heat.

I stroked my cock up and down his crack, coating it in his slick before finally pressing forward on his hole. Pitt's toes curled and he thrust his hips up to meet mine. I ground my hips against him, feeling as the head of my cock rolled over his prostate. I groaned as Pitt's body pulled me into the warm heat of his ass.

Pitt's eyes were rolled back in his head, and his mouth dropped open as a slurry of moans and groans fell from his lips. The sound of slapping skin bounced around the room as our hips pounded together. I stroked my hands up and down his body, paying close attention to every area that made him moan louder. My panther pushed closer to the front wanting to make our mate our own.

I held my panther back, edging out for as long as possible. I watched the minute that Pitt's bear took over. His eyes flared a dark brown, darker than I'd seen them. His incisors lengthened, and he leaned forward with a roar. The minute his teeth sunk into my chest, my knot swelled and locked us together. I cried out as pleasure washed over me, more potent than any orgasm I'd ever experienced.

My panther pushed through my hold, and my own incisors lengthened. I leaned forward and pierced Pitt's chest above his right nipple. Pitt cried out, and cum flooded over our stomachs. When his blood hit my tongue, I came again with a roar. My whole body tingled and when I opened my eyes to look down at Pitt, I realized something. I thought I was never going to come back to reality. This was what it was like to have love at first sight.

I'd never believed in it. That instant love bullshit was for romance novels. But it was like I'd met the man I could only dream of. Mother fate had sent him to me, and he was perfect for me in every way.

Pitt slowly opened his eyes, and a lazy smile formed on his lips.

"I love you," I blurted.

Pitt's eyes widened, and he gasped. I prepared myself for rejection, but Pitt surprised me when he leaned forward and kissed my lips briefly.

"I love you too. It's weird. How is that possible?"

I shook my head and shrugged. "I don't know. But it's like I've always known you. I don't know-how. But I feel like you've always been in my life."

"Yeah, I feel the same way. Maybe in a sense, we always have been in each other's lives. We just didn't know it. But we were always destined to be together."

A small smile formed on my lips, and I nodded my head. "That's quite the possibility. I wouldn't be shocked to find out that is true. Magic. It's an awesome thing."

Pitt giggled and nodded his head. "I'm learning, I like it more and more."

"I guess we do need to talk about some things, though. I probably should've talked about them before we did this," I said as I moved my hips to where my knot was still firmly locked.

"What do you want to talk about?"

"Well, for one, I need to know what you want? Like I know you live in Melbourne, and you wanted to travel. I can't travel with you, but I guess I can move. Not straight away, I'd have to organize someone to manage the shop for me," I began.

Pitt shook his head. "No. I don't want any of that. I did a lot of thinking, so I didn't have a decision until this morning. I wanted to make sure I was certain about the decision I made. I want to move here to Lalbert. We can travel when we are older. We have years yet."

A smile formed on my face. "You really want to move to Lalbert?"

Pitt nodded his head. "I don't know if Anghus would be alright with it, but I would like to move to the Devil's Advocates compound. I'd like to raise our children there with the other children."

My eyes widened as I realized children. I always knew that came with mating, but the real possibility of having children was here.

"Oh wow, I realized we might be fathers."

"I should've asked if you wanted children." Pitt chuckled. "I hope so," he replied before wincing.

"Oh, gods, yes. I want children. So many children."

"Woah. I'm not sure I want so many children," Pitt laughed.

I grinned and leaned forward, kissing him on the lips. I would happily have as many children as possible that Pitt was willing to give me. Even if that was only ever one.

Chapter Seventeen

P^itt

"Oh fuck, Obsidian, I'm going to cum, yes," I cried out as Obsidian pounded into me again for the eighth time over the last twenty-four hours.

"Cum, baby, I'm right behind you," Obsidian grunted as I felt his knot lock deep inside me. My eyes rolled, and I roared as cum sprayed across the sheets, and I felt the warmth of Obsidian's seed fill me.

"Oh gods, I don't know that I can go again after this," I said, breathing heavily.

Obsidian chuckled from behind me and kissed my naked shoulder. "We have been going at it all night. I'm surprised if Atticus wasn't run out of the house for the night."

My eyes widened, and I gasped. "Shit. I didn't think of Atticus. Do you think he wouldn't have come home?"

"Na. He probably went to stay with Stagger. The two of them are best friends and regularly stay together."

"I haven't met Stagger. I met Alena, Atticus, Donte, and Dakota on Friday."

"There is also Boden, but he is away at the moment. His Mama is ill and the only one she has left, so he had to take time off to look after her."

"Oh. I'm sorry to hear that. But giving him the time off makes you a great boss."

Obsidian shrugged his shoulders. "My employees are like family to me. Without them, I'd not be as busy or successful as I am."

I smiled at my mate. We'd talked a little bit in between our fuck sessions. I knew from Bacchus that Obsidian was the second youngest in a family of seven boys. We had spent the in-between time getting to know one another more.

Obsidian reached over to the bedside table and picked up his phone. "It's four in the morning," he chuckled. "Wanna get some sleep before we have to get up. Valerie's new engine is supposed to arrive today, and it would be good to talk to Anghus about getting a home out on the compound."

I smiled and nodded as a wave of exhaustion swept over me as if the mere mention of sleep was enough to kick my body into action.

"That sounds like a plan," I said sleepily. Obsidian chuckled and pressed another kiss to my shoulder but wrapped his arm around my waist and buried his head into my neck. I was drifting into sleep when I felt his knot unlock and his cock slip from inside me.

I couldn't believe this was my life. But I was going to love every minute of it. I couldn't wait to tell Dad and Papa about Obsidian.

• • • •

IT WAS NEARING LUNCHTIME when we finally woke. After a quick shower, followed by a very delicious blow job, we went to the shop, where we were greeted with wolf whistles and cheers. My cheeks tinted pink. But there were no nerves at all. In fact, my heart didn't even kick faster. It was like all I needed was Obsidian. I was happy. I was complete. I wasn't about to give up my regular medication, but I hoped that it meant that I could finally get rid of the Valium.

"Valerie's motor arrived this morning," Atticus said. "Stagger and Donte have made a start on the installation. I've got a brake and oil change to do, then I'll help them."

Obsidian nodded his head. "Thanks, man. I'm going to be back to help. I just want to take Pitt out to the compound, though, first. We decided it's the best place to get a house."

"Sure thing, man. I'll talk to you more when you get back," Atticus said with a wave as he turned back to the car he was working on.

Obsidian led me out of the shop and into the office space where Alena was busy dealing with a customer. She gave us a small wave and a wink as we passed but continued working with the customer she had. Once we reached Obsidian's car, I climbed into the passenger seat with a smile.

"This is a beautiful car," I said as I gently skimmed my fingers off the dash.

"She is my baby. I got her when I was eighteen. The first car I ever bought. She was a bomb when I bought her, but after much love and care, I got her up to her current state."

"That's amazing. Valerie was my first car too. Dad and Papa always bought us new cars when we turned eighteen and finished high school. They wanted to buy me a new car, but I saw Valerie and fell in love. It's who I wanted. Finally, after much persuading, Dad said yes, so she became mine. However, I haven't been able to put the same love and attention into her that you have for yours."

Obsidian shook his head as the car rumbled to life. "Don't stress. You are now mated to this really awesome mechanic that can make Valerie purr like a kitten."

I giggled as Obsidian pulled out of the carpark and headed towards the Devil's Advocates compound.

Chapter Eighteen

Obsidian

"Uncle Sid," Iver screeched as he came running down from the school building to where I parked my car.

"Nephew Iver," I replied with a laugh. "Are you meant to be outside, or are you supposed to be studying?"

Iver's grin was cheeky. "I was supposed to be going to the garden to work with Trudy because I'd finished all my work for the day, but then I saw you."

I chuckled. "Alright, get down the garden before your Dad comes and kicks my ass for distracting you."

"Dad would never do that," Iver said with a roll of his eyes before he turned to Pitt. "I'm glad you found your mate."

Pitt grinned and leaned into my side. "I'm glad too."

Iver turned and took off toward the garden where Trudy would be waiting for him. "Come on, let's go and chat with Anghus and Joachim. Bacchus will probably be at work."

Pitt nodded his head and followed me into the main house. Joachim was sitting on Anghus's lap as they kissed.

"Gross," I complained, causing Anghus to throw his head back and laugh.

"Dude, what are you even doing out of the bedroom?" he asked.

I chuckled. "I needed to give little Obsidian a rest for a few hours."

"Weak," Anghus replied with laughter.

"No, just need to pace me; I'm a marathon fucker, not a sprinter like some."

Anghus laughed so hard I thought he would fall out of the chair he was sitting in.

"Alright, alright. Iver said that you'd probably be around today. So, does this mean you will move to the compound?"

I glanced at Pitt, who looked at me with wide eyes that Anghus knew what to expect. There were no secrets where Iver was concerned.

"Yeah. Pitt said he felt really comfortable here. And the apartment won't work if we have kids."

Anghus nodded before tapping on Joachim's leg to get him to stand. Once Anghus was out of the chair, he pulled out a piece of paper that appeared to be a map of the compound.

"The plots highlighted in orange are the family homes that have been built already. The ones in green are the plots where houses could be built, so it's up to you whether you want to build your own place or move into one of the houses," Anghus said.

"I want to buy one from you, Anghus, you know that, don't you?" I said.

Anghus rolled his eyes. "I swear you Rigby's are a pain in the ass. None of you let me just give you something."

I chuckled. "It was how Mama and Papa raised us."

Anghus smiled and looked over at Pitt. "What would you rather, Pitt, build your own house or just move into one already built?"

"I don't mind, really. I'm more interested in where the property is," Pitt replied before looking over at me. "Of course, that's if you want to, but I'd really like to live near the creek. I felt the most at home there."

I smiled and nodded my head. "Of course, that's possible. I don't mind where we live as long as we are together."

"That's so gorgeous," Joachim gushed. "Remember when we were like that?"

Anghus snorted. "We are still like that."

Joachim rolled his eyes and put his hands on his hips. "Only when you are begging for another baby."

"Oh, still not on board?" I asked Joachim.

"I'm warming more to it, but I'm still thinking about it," he replied, causing Anghus's smile to grow.

I smirked and looked down at the map. "There are two houses that are built right next to the creek, and there are two more plots where we could build if you wanted," I said as I pointed out the properties to Pitt.

One of the properties was already taken by Freya and her mates. I knew they liked living at the back of the compound because of their lifestyle. The two empty blocks sat between their home and one of the built homes.

"Can we go and see the built homes? I think they would work well for us, and we can move in straight away," Pitt said.

"Sure, I can take you to look at them," Anghus said. "They are all three bedrooms, two bathrooms. You have a secured yard so the little ones can play without worrying about them going into the creek."

Pitt smiled. "I like the sound of that."

"Of course, if you want to change the color on the inside or do whatever to it, you can," Joachim said.

Pitt's smile was huge when he glanced at me and nodded his head. "I think that sounds perfect."

I leaned forward and pressed a kiss on Pitt's cheek. "Me too, baby."

Chapter Nineteen

P itt

The house was perfect, and I couldn't wait to move in. There was only one other occupied house on the back of the compound. A vampire named Freya lived there with her three mates, Miles, Creed, and Caden. Obsidian said that Freya worked for his brother Asher, who owned a kink club in town. Apparently, Freya was a Domme, and her three men were all submissive and into all sorts of kink.

I wasn't sure that was my life, but I definitely didn't judge them. Although I was intrigued when Anghus mentioned that Freya had a dungeon room in their house. I couldn't even fathom what you would put in a dungeon. But it sounded terrifying. Definitely not my kink.

By the time we had looked through the homes and picked which one we wanted, it was nearing late afternoon.

"Do you want to go and visit Mama and Papa?" Obsidian asked as we climbed into the car to leave the compound.

I felt my nerves instantly begin to kick up. I'd never met the parents of a partner before. Obsidian seemed to sense my nerves and reached out his hand, clasping mine.

"I promise that they are fantastic people. None of my brothers have completely normal mates. Macklin is mated to a man who was in a bombing attack while in the middle east and suffers from PTSD. Burgess's mate was burned to eighty percent of his body and also struggles with PTSD. Asher's mate March is a spider shifter and the youngest of twenty. And Drake and his partner both have HIV. Trust me, your anxiety won't cause them to bat an eyelid."

I gasped, and my eyes widened. "Wow, it's like Mother fate brought these people to you all because you are the healers."

Obsidian chuckled and nodded his head. "I'd never looked at it like that, but you might be onto something. Even Anghus and Joachim grew up in breeding facilities and Morpheus, so they needed healing too."

"There is definitely something in it," I said.

"I think it has to do with my Mama and Papa. Wait until you meet Mama, she loves everyone, and no one comes away feeling like they were unloved or cared for."

I smiled. "I like the sound of that. My Papa is very similar. I have to ring them and tell them about you yet."

Obsidian grinned. "Do you think they would like me?"

I chuckled and nodded my head. "Definitely. Papa loves all things cars. He will talk your ear off for hours. While Dad is more like Anghus, he is quiet but protective. My brothers and sister will adore you too, the same with my nephews and nieces."

"I can't wait to meet them. After we move into the new house, we should have everyone over, and we can meet them all. Especially now that Drake is living back in Australia, he and the kids with his mate Arsen will be there."

I smiled at my mate and nodded my head. "That sounds perfect."

• • • •

IT WAS PERFECT. THREE weeks later, Obsidian and I were moved into our house, and I was fussing around the kitchen with Abigail. She had become like a mother to me, her love just oozed from her. She didn't have to even try; it came so naturally. Obsidian had invited all his brothers, their mates and children, and those he worked with. While I'd asked my whole family.

Dad and Papa had been thrilled, although I think secretly that Talia might have told them. It didn't matter; they were excited and happy to know I'd found someone. Dad had even mentioned that I sounded so much more comfortable. I wasn't stuttering, and I'd even noticed that my anxiety was becoming less of an issue.

I'd started seeing a new psychologist who worked out of the compound, Alexandra. She was lovely. A human, but she had a vast understanding of supernaturals. She had got all my notes from Naomi and said that she could see from what Naomi had written that I was changing and becoming more assertive. I hoped that there would be a day that I would no longer need my medication, but I was happy just not to have the panic attacks like I was.

I still had them. Unfortunately, they were something that would stick with me for a while longer. But I didn't get them to the same ferocity or as often as I had been. Obsidian was excellent through them. He talked me through each attack and calmed me down. It was perfect.

To top off my wonderful new life, I'd discovered I was pregnant. I'd taken a pregnancy test, and we planned to tell everyone today. I couldn't wait to meet our little one. Obsidian wanted so many children; I wasn't sure I wanted that many, but I would definitely agree to maybe two or three. We would see.

<h1 style="text-align: right">Chapter Twenty</h1>

O bsidian

Everyone arrived just before lunch at our new house. I loved it. I'd never felt so fulfilled as I did now. I couldn't believe how lucky I'd become. I had a mate, a home I loved, and family surrounding me. Watching Pitt grow in confidence as he worked out of the compound was terrific. He'd taken to the garden with a green thumb of a gnome. He and Trudy were fast becoming best friends. Even his anxiety was becoming less. He didn't stutter as often and didn't get anxious. I was proud of him and all the changes that were happening.

Not to mention I was about to become a Dad. I couldn't believe how lucky I'd got.

"Obsidian, I'd like you to meet my Dad and Papa, Udo and Oscar," Pitt said as he walked towards me with two men flanking him. There was no denying who Pitt's Dad was. He was identical to him, right down to the same flare of seriousness in his eyes.

"It's wonderful to meet you both," I said as I held my hand out to shake them.

"It's great to meet you too, Obsidian," Oscar said. "Pitt has told us so much about you that I couldn't wait for today."

I chuckled. "Hopefully, he told you good things, not about how I leave my undies on the ground."

Pitt giggled and shook his head. "You're getting better."

I grinned as several other people, including children, joined us.

"This is the rest of my family. This is my sister Talia. My brother Nathan and his mate Christopher. And my other brother, Carson. And these terrors are my nephews and nieces, Nathan and Christopher's children. They are Jude, Reed, Kiara, Lexi, Rory, and Bailey."

I grinned. "See, it's in the genes to have big families," I said with a laugh.

Pitt rolled his eyes, but I saw the slight smile on his face. I knew that I was wearing him down. Although I should probably wait until after he gave birth for the first time before trying to convince him to have a huge family.

"These are my parents, Abigail and Lionel," I introduced as Mama and Papa came to join us.

My parents shook hands with everyone and started to chat amongst themselves. When I looked around again, I saw Iver coming over to me.

"Hey, Uncle Sid," he said with a smile before turning his attention to the kids. "Hi, my name is Iver. Want to come and play with my cousins?"

The kids all nodded their heads and took off to play whatever game the kids were all playing.

I slung my arm around Pitt's shoulders and kissed his cheek. "I could get used to having all of our families around."

Pitt smiled and nodded his head. "I could too. I'm glad that Dad and Papa are only a few hours down the road, which makes it easier to visit."

I nodded and stared out at everyone. They all seemed so happy. Suddenly there was a loud gasp behind me, and I turned to see what was happening. Pitt's brother Carson was standing staring at Stagger, who'd just come in with Atticus.

"What's wrong? What's going on?" Pitt asked with confusion as Carson stood looking at Stagger with wide eyes.

Atticus chuckled and slapped Stagger on the back, who looked just as dumbfounded as Carson.

"My mate," Carson whispered.

"How?" Stagger muttered. "We are both alphas."

"So are Bacchus and Anghus, but they worked it out," I said.

"Holy shit," Stagger said as he walked towards Carson. "I'm Stagger."

"I'm Carson. You really are my mate?"

"Yeah, it appears so."

I couldn't stop watching the making of another relationship. I was so excited to see it happen. Stagger had come from a complex home. He was born into Morpheus and made to breed with omegas before the Onyx Rebels rescued him. He was always determined that he would never mate with anyone. Yet sometimes, Mother fate just brought them all together.

"Um, Carson," Talia said.

Carson blinked and turned to his sister, who leaned in close, but I could easily understand what she said because she was close to us.

"Go fuck your mate," she whispered. I snorted a laugh as Carson blinked and looked around at everyone standing close by and watching the two discover each other.

"Do you want to be my mate?" Stagger asked.

Carson licked over his bottom lip and nodded his head.

Stagger reached out his hand, and when Carson took Stagger's hand, I could have sworn there were electric pulses running through them both. Mother fate had done a great job again.

"The spare bedroom is made up if you can't make it back to your place," I said to Stagger, who nodded his head but didn't say anything more as he led an equally speechless Carson into the house.

I chuckled and glanced at Pitt, watching his brother with pride.

"Well, that was unexpected," Udo said with a chuckle.

"Can't deny Mother fate when she comes calling," Mama said with a laugh.

"That you can't, Abigail, that you can't."

Chapter Twenty-One

P itt

It was nearing dinner time when Stagger and Carson re-emerged from the spare room. Carson's cheeks were tinted pink as he came down the back stairs.

"Sorry for messing up your day Pitt," he said quietly.

I shook my head and opened my arms to embrace my brother. "You did no such thing. I'm happy for you."

Carson looked at me and smiled. "Yeah?"

"Yeah. I've got to know Stagger over the last few weeks; he is an adorable guy."

Carson's smile grew, and he nodded his head. "He appears to be."

"Are you going to move to Lalbert?" I asked.

Carson bit into his bottom lip. "Yeah. I have to give notice at home before moving up here, but Stagger said he would take some time off and come to help me move."

"That's awesome. I'm looking forward to having you up here."

"It will be good knowing someone before I move."

I nodded my head. Carson was much more extroverted than I was, and it never seemed hard for him to make friends but moving to a new town was scary.

"Hey baby, now that Carson and Stagger are back, do you want to make the announcement?" Obsidian asked as he wrapped his arm around my waist and pulled me into his chest.

I nodded my head. I wasn't sure whether to wait for Carson and Stagger or to just make the announcement without them, but the way it worked out was perfect. Having my brother here with his mate made it even better.

"Excuse me, everyone," Obsidian called. Slowly everyone stopped talking and turned to look at Obsidian. "First of all, I'd like to thank everyone for coming and celebrating with us in true Rigby style. I've had a wonderful time meeting Pitt's family and look forward to getting to know you all the better over the coming years. And, of course, a massive thank you needs to be said to Mama. Without her lasagna, I'm not sure it would be a decent cookout."

Abigail laughed and waved her hand off at Obsidian, who grinned at his Mama. Although I had to admit, Abigail's lasagna was hands down the best-tasting dish I'd ever experienced. I could definitely get used to eating that regularly.

"Pitt and I would like to make an announcement, one that I'm sure many of you have already guessed and that Iver already knows," Obsidian said, grinning at his nephew. The returning of the latter smile was full of mischief and knowledge. That boy blew my mind the more I got to know him. "But we are expecting a baby."

A cheer sounded throughout the backyard at the news. Carson pulled me into his arms and kissed my cheek. My face heated with the attention.

"Congratulations, Pitt. You are going to make the best Papa," he said enthusiastically.

"Thank you," I grinned. "I can't wait to meet them."

Everyone came up to us and kissed and cuddled Obsidian and me while congratulating us. I couldn't believe how exciting this was. Once everyone had finished saying their congratulations and were getting ready to pack up and go, I saw Iver walking towards me with a slight smile on his lips.

"You knew, didn't you?" I asked.

Iver grinned and bounced his head up and down. "I know whenever someone is pregnant."

"How?"

Iver shrugged his shoulders. "At first, I thought it was the creator that sent me messages, but then I realized it was in the scent. Your scent changes when you get pregnant, and I can tell."

"Obsidian said that you've always been able to tell the gender of the baby and their name too."

Iver nodded his head. "That comes from connecting with the baby's spirit. I can communicate with them while they are still growing. I can see them and know what they will look like and what supernatural they are destined to be."

My eyes widened, and my mouth dropped open. "Are you serious?"

Iver's grin widened as he nodded enthusiastically. "Do you want to know?"

I bit my lip as I thought about whether this was the knowledge I wanted now or if I wanted to wait. We were going to be having an ultrasound not terribly far away.

"I tell you what, write it down on paper. The gender and the name. Then when we have our ultrasound, I'll give it to the radiologist to confirm."

Iver giggled and nodded his head. "Okay, I can do that," he said as he turned and ran from the yard into the house. Not even five minutes later, he came back with a sealed envelope. "Here you go, Uncle Pitt."

I took the envelope and bent down to kiss Iver on the cheek. I couldn't believe just how lucky I was to be brought into this family that was not only so welcoming but so healing at the same time.

Chapter Twenty-Two

O bsidian

"Pitt and Obsidian Rigby," Reagan called. "Dear God, someone actually managed to put up with you, huh?"

I barked out a laugh. "I'm fortunate," I replied, taking Pitt's hand.

"Hi, Pitt. I'm Reagan. I went to school with Obsidian and practically grew up with the Rigby family. It's lovely to meet you, and I'm so glad that the two of you are mated. I will tell you a secret, Obsidian has wanted to be mated since he knew what it was."

Pitt looked at me with wide eyes and gasped. "Really?"

I shrugged my shoulders. "It's true. It was the one thing I wanted, other than being a mechanic."

"Then it's me that is lucky," Pitt said as he squeezed my hand.

"I think you are both lucky," Reagan said with a sigh. I knew that she was still single. I had always wondered if she and one of the medics, Kaylee, were fated, but nothing ever seemed to happen with that. "Alright, let's get you on the table so we can look at the bub."

Pitt climbed on the table and laid flat on his back. I had been looking forward to this day about as much as I'd been looking forward to the birth. We'd all taken bets as to what the gender would be. Me, Macklin, and Drake believed we were going to have a girl. While the others thought it was a boy. I'd wondered if Bacchus had cheated and asked Iver, but he promised he hadn't.

"I'm going to just spread some goop on your belly, and then we will have a look. Do you want to know the gender?" Reagan asked.

"Yes. I have an envelope from my nephew Iver; he has written his prediction, so we are hoping you can confirm it before telling us," Pitt said.

Reagan grinned. "I know, Iver. He is a cute kid. The last time I saw him in the street with Bacchus and Joachim, he told me that I would have a mate coming to me soon; they are just a little stuck in their head now."

"Iver told me I was going to meet Pitt too. Then I scented his car and knew we were mates."

Reagan looked at me with confusion. "I don't know how you scented a car, but I'm glad. Right, there is definitely only one baby in here. That is their heartbeat there," she said as she pointed at the screen. "I'll just take my measurements, and then we can confirm Iver's prediction." Reagan began to move the wand around and clicking on the keyboard as she took various measurements of the baby. "Bubs is very healthy. You do have a thick amniotic sac, but other than that everything seems to be completely normal."

"Will that affect the baby?" I asked.

Reagan shook her head. "No. It just might mean that Pitt's waters might have to be broken before he can give birth, other than that the baby will be fine. Of course, there are things that can go wrong with child birth, but generally nowadays everything is a lot better medically."

I smiled at Reagan and nodded my head. I couldn't wait for the chance to meet our baby. But the thought of something going wrong was a real concern.

After a few more clicks on the keyboard Reagan turned to Pitt. "Got the envelope?" she asked.

Pitt nodded and handed Reagan the envelope in which Iver had sealed his prediction. She tore it open and read the piece of paper with a smile.

"Well, Iver has done it again," she laughed. "Want to know?"

"Yes, please," Pitt answered. I leaned forward in my seat with excitement.

"You are definitely having a little girl," Reagan said.

I threw my hands up in the air and cheered. "Jericho owes me fifty bucks," I laughed.

Pitt and Reagan cackled at my antics. "What did Iver say her name was?" Pitt asked.

"Juniper. He even put down what supernatural she would be. Do you want to know that too?"

"Sure, why not," I said.

"A snow leopard."

Pitt grinned. "She is going to be the perfect combination between the two of us."

"What supernatural are you, Pitt. I can scent you're a shifter," Reagan asked.

"I'm a polar bear shifter."

"Oh yep, that is perfect then. And I adore her name."

Pitt nodded his head and looked over at me. "She will be perfect."

I leaned down and kissed my mate on the lips. "She will be," I said. I couldn't wait to have the opportunity to meet our daughter and then make more and more babies in the future.

"What do you think of a winter wonderland bedroom?" Pitt asked as we drove home. "I've been talking to Burgess and March; they want to paint the nursery."

"I love that idea. Our little snow queen. We have to include pine trees with juniper berries on them."

Pitt giggled and nodded his head. "We sure do."

I couldn't wait to get home. Not just to be able to make a start on the nursery but to also reveal the surprise I'd been working on for over a month. As it turned out, Valerie needed much more work than we had first expected. But I'd put all my spare time into fixing her up. As we pulled into the driveway, a grin crept across my face as Pitt gasped.

"Oh my god, Valerie," he said as he spun in the seat to stare at me. "You said that she was dust."

"I might've lied," I replied as I stopped the car and killed the engine.

Pitt ripped off his seatbelt and practically threw himself over the center of the car to wrap his arms around my neck and plant kisses on my face.

"Thank you so much. I love you," he said between kisses causing me to laugh.

"Come on, let's go and check her out."

Pitt leaped out of the car and walked to Valerie with the broadest smile on his face. He held his arms out and laid his chest on the bonnet as if giving the vehicle a hug. We'd done a lot of work, including having her resprayed and all the rust cut out of her. She now purred like a kitten and looked as beautiful as the day she came off the factory floor.

"Are you happy?" I asked with a chuckle.

Pitt looked at me with wide eyes. "Are you kidding? I'm in love. I'm ecstatic. I'm everything amazing."

"Yeah, you are, baby, yeah you are."

P^{itt}
 "Oh my god, oh my god, oh my fucking god," Pitt groaned as he rocked back and forth in my arms. "How much longer is this going to take?"

"Until she decides to make her entrance, baby."

"It's been twelve hours already," he groaned.

Pitt's labor had been anything but easy. His water broke as he finished cleaning the windows; he'd become a clean-a-holic in the last few weeks. Mama said he was nesting and that it was completely normal. The contractions had started not long after that. At first, the contractions weren't too bad; they were not that close together, and the pain was manageable. But now we were heading into the thirteenth hour, and Pitt was exhausted and in pain. The contractions seemed to be coming one on top of the other.

I felt helpless. I wanted to be able to take away the pain from my mate, but there wasn't anything I could do. He had to ride it through.

Pitt let out another groan, and his arms tightened around my neck. We'd started off lying in bed, but then Dr. Rankin had suggested that we stand and walk as it sometimes helped the baby come faster.

"I don't know how much longer I can do this, Obsidian," Pitt groaned.

When I looked down at him, he had tears in his eyes. He'd been so brave. Pitt had decided from the moment we found out he was pregnant that he didn't want pain relief and wanted very little medical assistance. He was happy to have Juniper in the hospital but wanted it to go naturally. I guess he wasn't planning on it taking so long.

"That's okay, baby. If you want to get some medication, then do that. There is nothing wrong with that," I said with encouragement.

Pitt nodded his head but groaned as another contraction took over. Once he'd moved through the contraction, I slowly walked him over to the bed and pressed the button on the buzzer.

A nurse came into the room with a smile. "How's it going?" she asked.

"He isn't coping very well with the pain right now; I was just hoping to see if we can do a check on him and see whether we could get some pain meds," I said, just as Pitt let out another groan.

"Of course. Pitt, do you want to remain to stand, or would you be more comfortable sitting on a bed?"

Pitt shook his head. "No. I'll stand. I feel like the baby's head is right there; if I sit, I will squish her."

The nurse chuckled as she put some gloves on. "The feeling of her head down low could be a good sign; it might mean that she is ready to start coming out. I'm just going to have a little look." The nurse walked behind Pitt and knelt down. "Oh shit."

"Oh, shit, what?" I said with fear.

"It's alright, the baby is just having a little trouble coming out because she was in a double sac," the nurse said with concern. "Pitt, don't push for me for a minute; I need to try and break the waters."

Tears fell from Pitt's eyes. My heart was racing as I wondered if we'd missed something. I looked behind Pitt but couldn't see anything.

"Obsidian, I'll get you to press that buzzer three long times, please," the nurse instructed.

I did as she said and watched in horror as soon doctors and nurses seemed to come from everywhere, wheeling in all equipment and talking over each other. I didn't know what was going on and the fear I felt was overwhelming.

"Pitt?" I asked. My mate's eyes were closed tight, and a steady stream trekked down over his cheeks. "It's going to be alright, Pitt."

Pitt shook his head, and I could see his whole-body trembling under the weight of his anxiety.

"Please do something," I said, looking between the nurses and doctors.

Dr. Rankin smiled tenderly at me. "It's going to be alright. The baby seems fine; she is encased in a second amniotic sac so we will have to break the waters. But Pitt, I need you to do your best to climb onto the bed on your knees for me."

Pitt nodded his head, and as he held my arm, I helped him to climb onto the bed. I was finally able to see Pitt's birth canal. Our daughter looked like she was trapped inside a plastic bag. Her face was smooshed and not entirely out of Pitt. My heart was ricocheting against my chest. *How could this happen? How didn't we notice?* Pitt hadn't mentioned anything about needing to push. I was so confused and the more I looked at my daughter the more concern I felt. This wasn't normal. There was something very wrong.

"Pitt, I want you to bear down with the next contraction," Dr. Rankin instructed. "I want some shifter blood bags on hand."

Nurses were running in and out of the room; some were carrying blankets, bags of blood, and instruments. Pitt made an animalistic cry as he pushed, and I watched our baby fall into the nurse's arms.

"Alright, let's get him onto his back," Dr. Rankin said. Nurses quickly helped Pitt onto his back, and I watched in horror as a large gush of blood poured from my mate. His face paled, and his eyes rolled. In the background I heard our daughter cry out and looked over to see the nurse cutting away the bag she'd been born in. But my mate was unconscious and there was blood pouring from him so much it was running off the bed and onto the floor.

"Pitt," I screamed.

"Obsidian, you need to come out for a moment. We are going to do everything we can to make him better," a nurse said to me.

"No," I screamed. "I'm not leaving my mate."

"Obsidian, you will leave now," Dr. Rankin growled, letting his alpha ripple enough that I had no choice but obey.

I walked out of the room with tears streaming down my cheeks and panic in my chest so tight that I thought I would suffocate.

"Sid," Bacchus called as he came running down the hallway, followed by my brothers. They pulled me into their arms and held me as I sobbed. I didn't know how they knew, but it didn't matter. All that mattered was my mate might be dying and I couldn't do anything to prevent it.

We were left in the waiting area for what felt like hours. Mama and Papa had joined us along with Pitt's family. We all wore the same look on our faces. Fear, worry, and grief. None of us knew anything. No one told us anything. And when someone asked, they were told they were working on Juniper and Pitt.

Finally, Dr. Rankin entered the waiting room, and I stood. He smiled and reached out a hand to clasp my arm.

"Is this all of Pitt's family, too?" he asked.

I looked at the faces that showed the same worry as mine did and nodded my head.

"Alright. Pitt is currently stable. However, we had to do surgery to remove his birth sac. It is very rare, but I've seen a few omegas; when they get pregnant, the baby, which is normally encased in an amniotic sac, will be held in a second sac. However, like in this case with Pitt, it isn't picked up in the ultrasound. It looks just like a thicker amniotic sac which is quite normal. Also, because Pitt's waters had broken it was assumed that meant there had been only one sac. In cases like this it's that outer sac that breaks and there is only a small amount of amniotic fluid that is released, and the baby will sometimes be born in the second sac. The skin of the second sac is harder and very similar to a finger nail that has been soaked for a long time in water. Unfortunately, that also means that it tears the placenta from the wall of the birth sac and therefore, the omega hemorrhages. This is what happened to Pitt. However, thankfully he was here in the hospital, and we were able to give him blood and remove the birth sac before he bled out."

Dr. Rankin's words were going into my head, but all I could think was that Pitt was stable. My mate was still alive.

"Juniper?" I asked.

"Is quite healthy. Thankfully we were able to get to her in time, and she was born very healthy at just a little over six pounds."

I breathed out a sigh of relief. "Can I see her?"

"Of course, I'll have one of the nurses bring her out to you so that you can all see her. As for Pitt, he is going to be very sore and tired until he can shift. But other than that, he will make a full recovery. However, I'm afraid that he won't be able to have any more children."

"I understand," I said. Although it was a blow, in the long run, it didn't matter. As long as my daughter and mate were alive and healthy, that was all I cared about.

A few minutes after Dr. Rankin left, a nurse wheeled a bassinet into the waiting area with a smile, and I got my first look at my daughter. She was beautiful. She had dark hair the same as me, with the same brown eyes as Pitt. She was the perfect combination. Juniper was passed around and kissed and cuddled by everyone before I took her back and walked with her into the room where Pitt was recovering.

Juniper let out a little squeal as if she knew Pitt was her Papa the minute, I laid her on his chest. Pitt's eyes slowly opened, and he looked up at me.

"Hey baby, Juniper is on your chest," I said.

Pitt looked down at our daughter with so much love on his face; I knew she would be the most spoiled and cared for little girl that could ever exist. I couldn't wait to get her face tattooed on the centre of my chest. I'd always kept that spot blank for the hopes that one day I would have a child to add there.

"I'm so lucky," Pitt whispered as he kissed the top of Juniper's head. "Me too, baby, me too."

The end.

Don't miss out!

Visit the website below and you can sign up to receive emails whenever S L Davies publishes a new book. There's no charge and no obligation.

https://books2read.com/r/B-A-NZRR-JEFBC

BOOKS 2 READ

Connecting independent readers to independent writers.

Also by S L Davies

Breeding Facility
Memphis
Bacchus
Coltrane
Pax
Raiden
Nash

Devil's Advocates
Lynx
Israel
Jai
Jasper
Arley
Zion
Oakland

KINK
Gunner
Newlyn

Freya
Tanquil

Obsidian Mechanics
Donte

Onyx Rebels
Onyx Rebels Prologue
Hawke

Rigby Brothers
Asher
Burgess
Macklin
Drake
Obsidian

Schiavu
Schiavu

Shifter Ink
Brenton
Chase
Orion

Standalone
Sisters Revenge
Killer Love
Soldiers At War
Second Chances
Bunny
Caged

Watch for more at https://www.amazon.com/~/e/B0832T8F7Z.

About the Author

S L Davies is an Australian Author living in Country, Victoria. She is inspired by the world around her.

Read more at https://www.amazon.com/~/e/B0832T8F7Z.

www.ingramcontent.com/pod-product-compliance
Lightning Source LLC
Chambersburg PA
CBHW031439130726
47989CB00003B/1209

9 798201 045678